THE PICTURE OF DORIAN GRAY

Adapted by

Daniel Conner

Illustrated by

Chris Allen

Based upon the works of

Oscar Wilde

magic
wagon

visit us at
www.abdopublishing.com

Published by Magic Wagon, a division of the ABDO Publishing Group, 8000 West 78th Street, Edina, Minnesota 55439. Copyright © 2010 by Abdo Consulting Group, Inc. International copyrights reserved in all countries. All rights reserved. No part of this book may be reproduced in any form without written permission from the publisher.

Graphic Planet™ is a trademark and logo of Magic Wagon.

Printed in the United States.

 Manufactured with paper containing at least 10% post-consumer waste

Original novel by Oscar Wilde
Adapted by Daniel Conner
Illustrated by Chris Allen
Colored by GURU-eFX
Lettered by Joeming Dunn
Edited by Stephanie Hedlund and Rochelle Baltzer
Interior layout and design by Antarctic Press
Cover art by Chris Allen
Cover design by Neil Klinepier

Library of Congress Cataloging-in-Publication Data

Conner, Daniel 1985-
    The picture of Dorian Gray / adapted by Daniel Conner; illustrated by Chris Allen; based upon the works of Oscar Wilde.
    p. cm. -- (Graphic planet. Graphic horror)
    Summary: A graphic novel based on the Oscar Wilde classic, in which an incredibly handsome young man in Victorian England retains his youthful appearance over the years while his portrait reflects both his age and evil soul as he pursues a life of decadence and corruption.
    ISBN 978-1-60270-680-4 (alk. paper)
    1. Graphic novels. [1. Graphic novels. 2. Conduct of life--Fiction. 3. Supernatural--Fiction. 4. Portraits--Fiction. 5. London (England)--History--1800-1950--Fiction. 6. Great Britain--History--Victoria, 1837-1901--Fiction. 7. Wilde, Oscar, 1854-1900. Picture of Dorian Gray--Adaptations. 8. Youths' writings.] I. Allen, Chris, 1972- ill. II. Wilde, Oscar, 1854-1900. Picture of Dorian Gray. III. Title.

PZ7.7.C66Pic 2010
741.5'973--dc22

2009008597

TABLE OF CONTENTS

The Picture of Dorian Gray..........4

About the Author........................31

Additional Works.......................31

Glossary...................................32

Web Sites..................................32

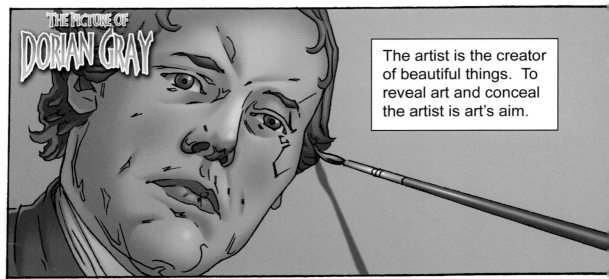

THE PICTURE OF DORIAN GRAY

The artist is the creator of beautiful things. To reveal art and conceal the artist is art's aim.

IT'S YOUR BEST WORK, BASIL. YOU MUST REALLY SEND IT NEXT YEAR TO THE GROSVENOR.

I DON'T THINK I SHALL SEND IT ANYWHERE. I HAVE PUT TOO MUCH OF MYSELF INTO IT.

EVERY PORTRAIT PAINTED WITH FEELING IS A PORTRAIT OF THE ARTIST, NOT OF THE SITTER. DORIAN GRAY IS TO ME SIMPLY A MOTIVE IN ART.

DORIAN GRAY? I MUST SEE HIM.

I DON'T WANT YOU TO MEET HIM. DORIAN GRAY IS MY DEAREST FRIEND. MY LIFE AS AN ARTIST DEPENDS ON HIM.

WHAT NONSENSE!

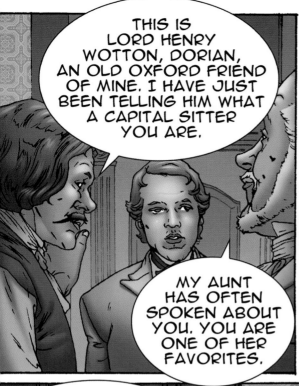

THIS IS LORD HENRY WOTTON, DORIAN, AN OLD OXFORD FRIEND OF MINE. I HAVE JUST BEEN TELLING HIM WHAT A CAPITAL SITTER YOU ARE.

MY AUNT HAS OFTEN SPOKEN ABOUT YOU. YOU ARE ONE OF HER FAVORITES.

HARRY, I WANT TO FINISH THIS PICTURE TODAY. WOULD YOU THINK IT AWFULLY RUDE OF ME IF I ASKED YOU TO GO AWAY?

IF DORIAN WISHES IT, OF COURSE YOU MUST STAY.

OH, PLEASE DON'T, LORD HENRY. BASIL IS IN ONE OF HIS SULKY MOODS, AND I CAN'T BEAR HIM WHEN HE SULKS.

HAVE YOU REALLY A VERY BAD INFLUENCE, LORD HENRY? AS BAD AS BASIL SAYS?

THE AIM OF LIFE IS SELF-DEVELOPMENT. THEY HAVE FORGOTTEN THE HIGHEST OF ALL DUTIES, THE DUTY THAT ONE OWES TO ONE'S SELF.

STOP! THERE IS SOME ANSWER TO YOU, BUT I CANNOT FIND IT. LET ME THINK.

For nearly ten minutes he stood there, motionless. The few words that Basil's friend had said to him had touched some secret chord that had never been touched before.

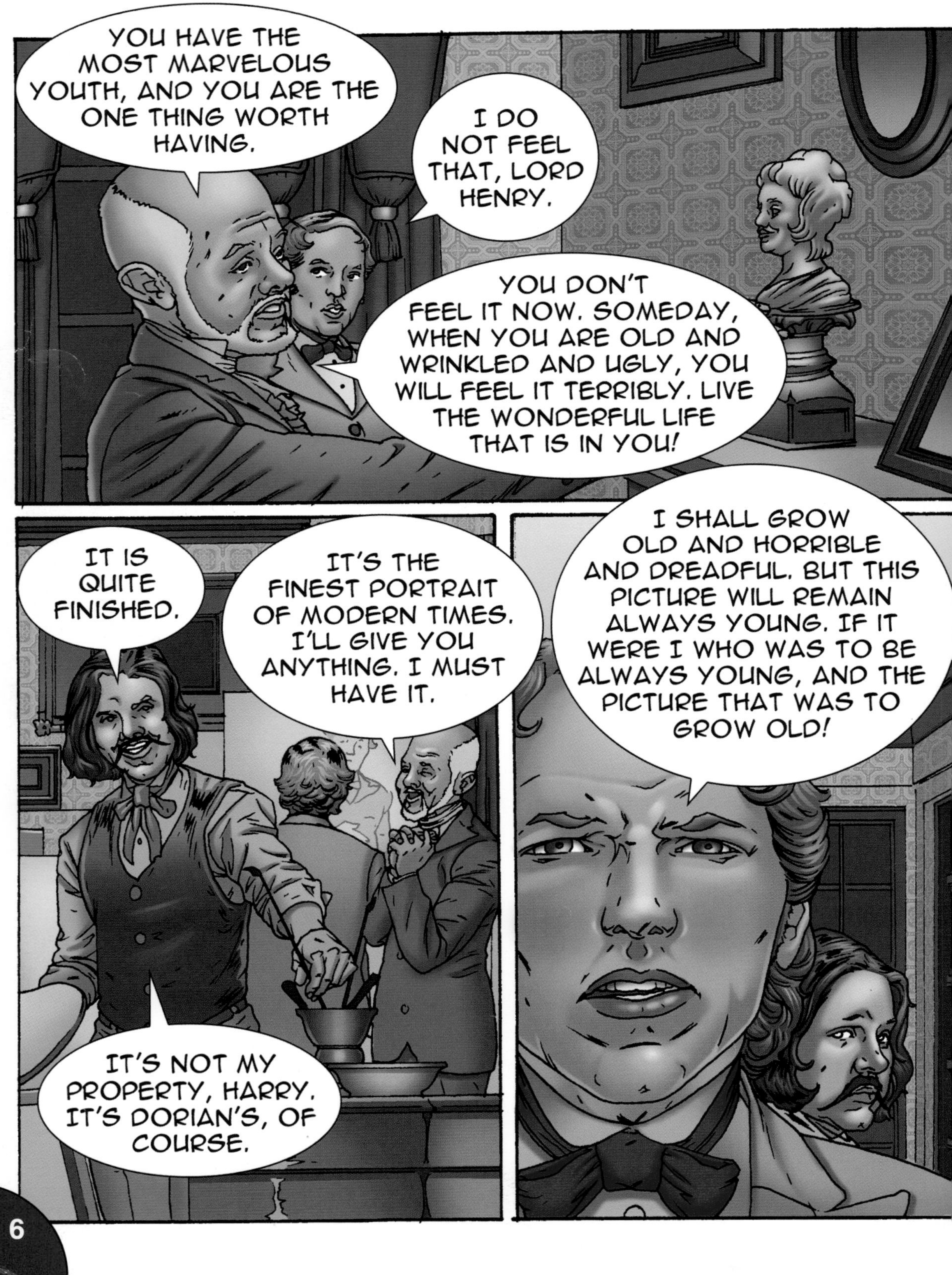
YOU HAVE THE MOST MARVELOUS YOUTH, AND YOU ARE THE ONE THING WORTH HAVING.
I DO NOT FEEL THAT, LORD HENRY.
YOU DON'T FEEL IT NOW. SOMEDAY, WHEN YOU ARE OLD AND WRINKLED AND UGLY, YOU WILL FEEL IT TERRIBLY. LIVE THE WONDERFUL LIFE THAT IS IN YOU!
IT IS QUITE FINISHED.
IT'S THE FINEST PORTRAIT OF MODERN TIMES. I'LL GIVE YOU ANYTHING. I MUST HAVE IT.
IT'S NOT MY PROPERTY, HARRY. IT'S DORIAN'S, OF COURSE.
I SHALL GROW OLD AND HORRIBLE AND DREADFUL. BUT THIS PICTURE WILL REMAIN ALWAYS YOUNG. IF IT WERE I WHO WAS TO BE ALWAYS YOUNG, AND THE PICTURE THAT WAS TO GROW OLD!

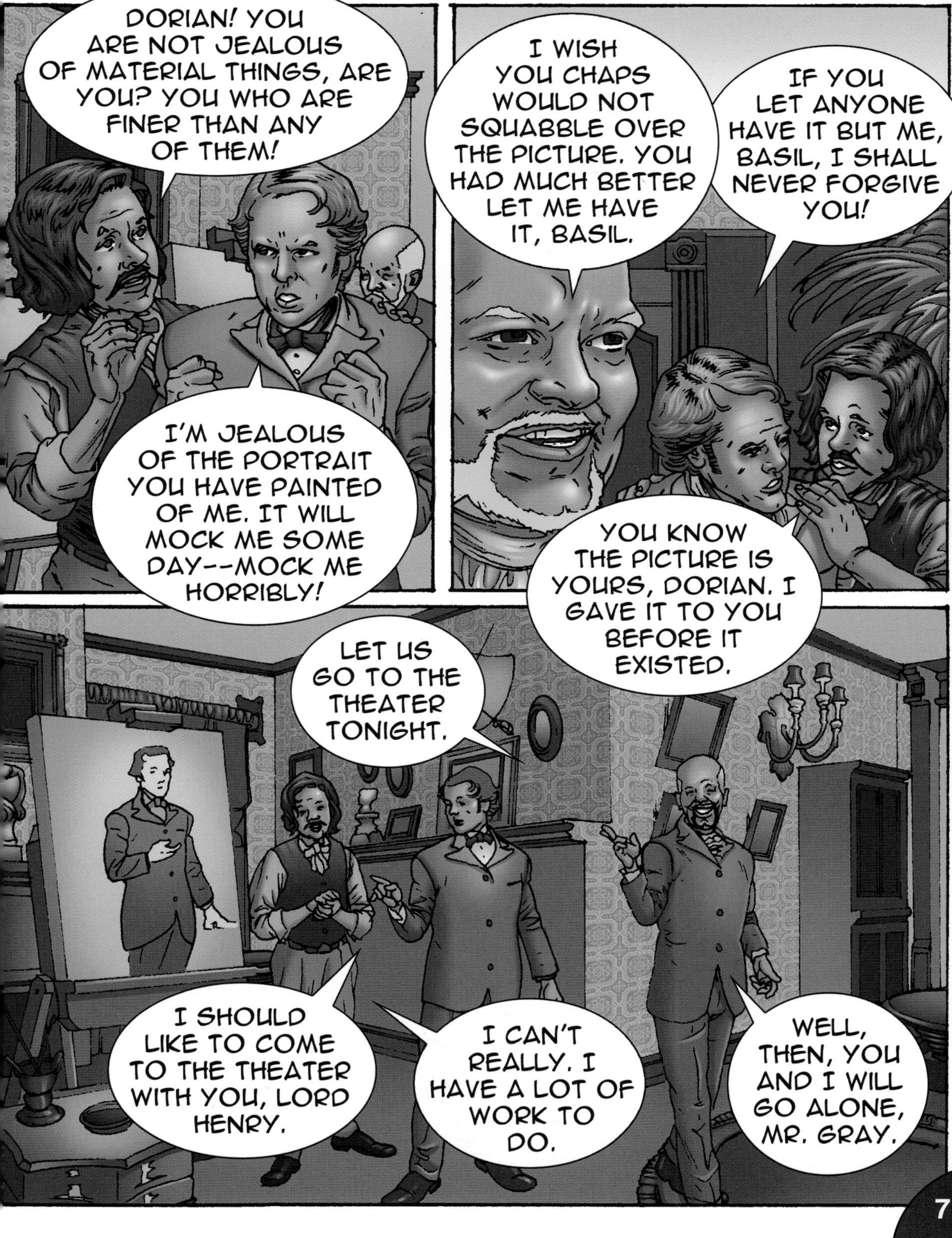
DORIAN! YOU ARE NOT JEALOUS OF MATERIAL THINGS, ARE YOU? YOU WHO ARE FINER THAN ANY OF THEM!
I'M JEALOUS OF THE PORTRAIT YOU HAVE PAINTED OF ME. IT WILL MOCK ME SOME DAY--MOCK ME HORRIBLY!
I WISH YOU CHAPS WOULD NOT SQUABBLE OVER THE PICTURE. YOU HAD MUCH BETTER LET ME HAVE IT, BASIL.
IF YOU LET ANYONE HAVE IT BUT ME, BASIL, I SHALL NEVER FORGIVE YOU!
YOU KNOW THE PICTURE IS YOURS, DORIAN. I GAVE IT TO YOU BEFORE IT EXISTED.
LET US GO TO THE THEATER TONIGHT.
I SHOULD LIKE TO COME TO THE THEATER WITH YOU, LORD HENRY.
I CAN'T REALLY. I HAVE A LOT OF WORK TO DO.
WELL, THEN, YOU AND I WILL GO ALONE, MR. GRAY.

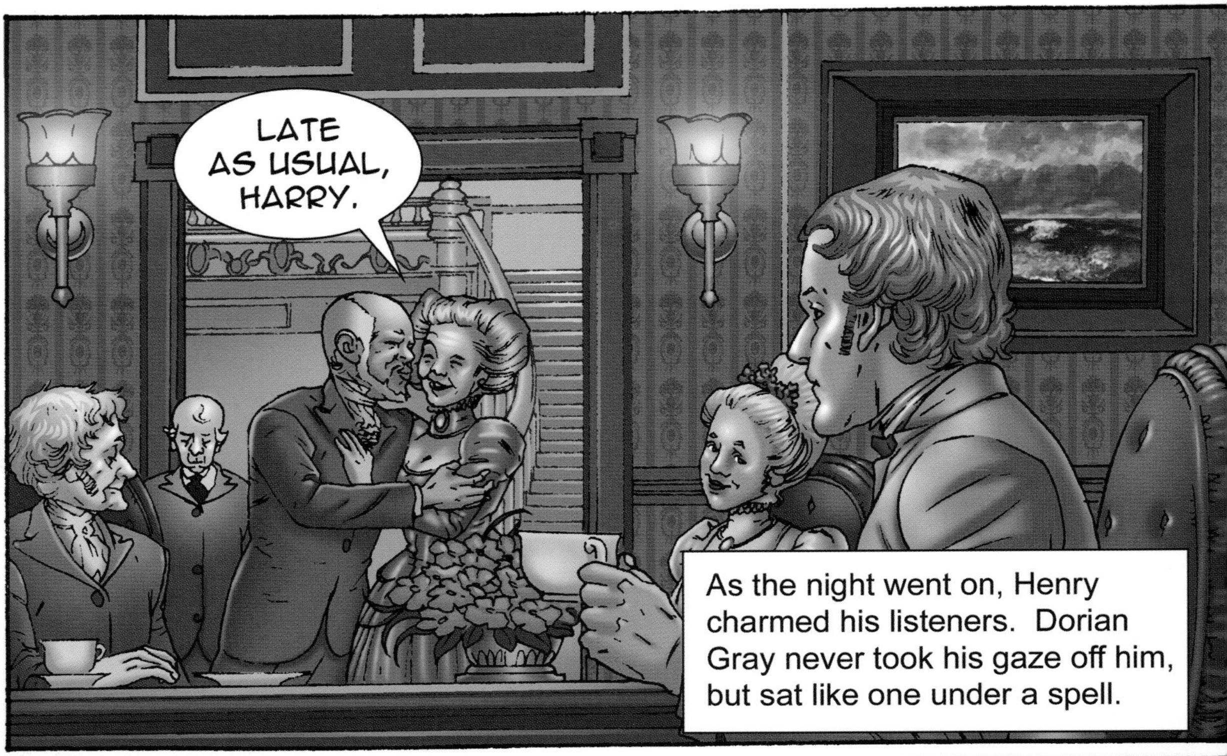
LATE AS USUAL, HARRY.
As the night went on, Henry charmed his listeners. Dorian Gray never took his gaze off him, but sat like one under a spell.

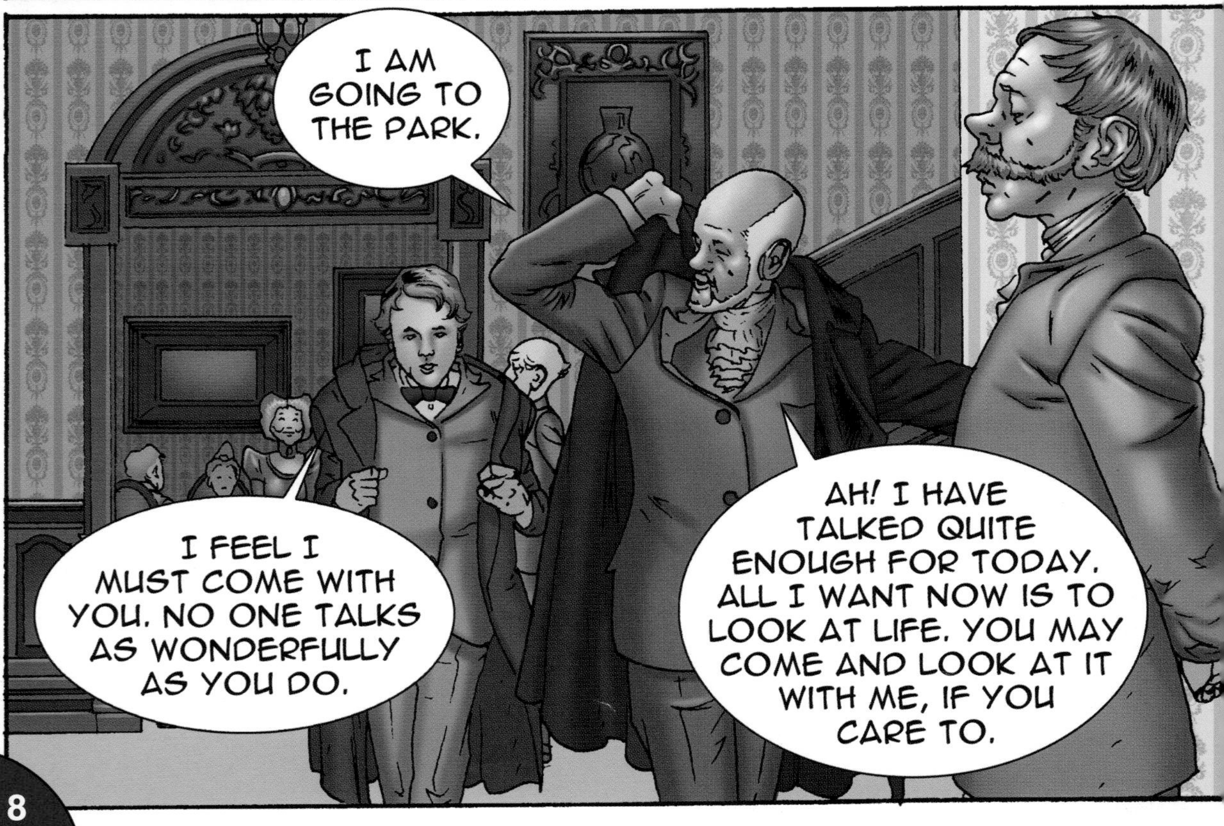
I AM GOING TO THE PARK.
I FEEL I MUST COME WITH YOU. NO ONE TALKS AS WONDERFULLY AS YOU DO.
AH! I HAVE TALKED QUITE ENOUGH FOR TODAY. ALL I WANT NOW IS TO LOOK AT LIFE. YOU MAY COME AND LOOK AT IT WITH ME, IF YOU CARE TO.

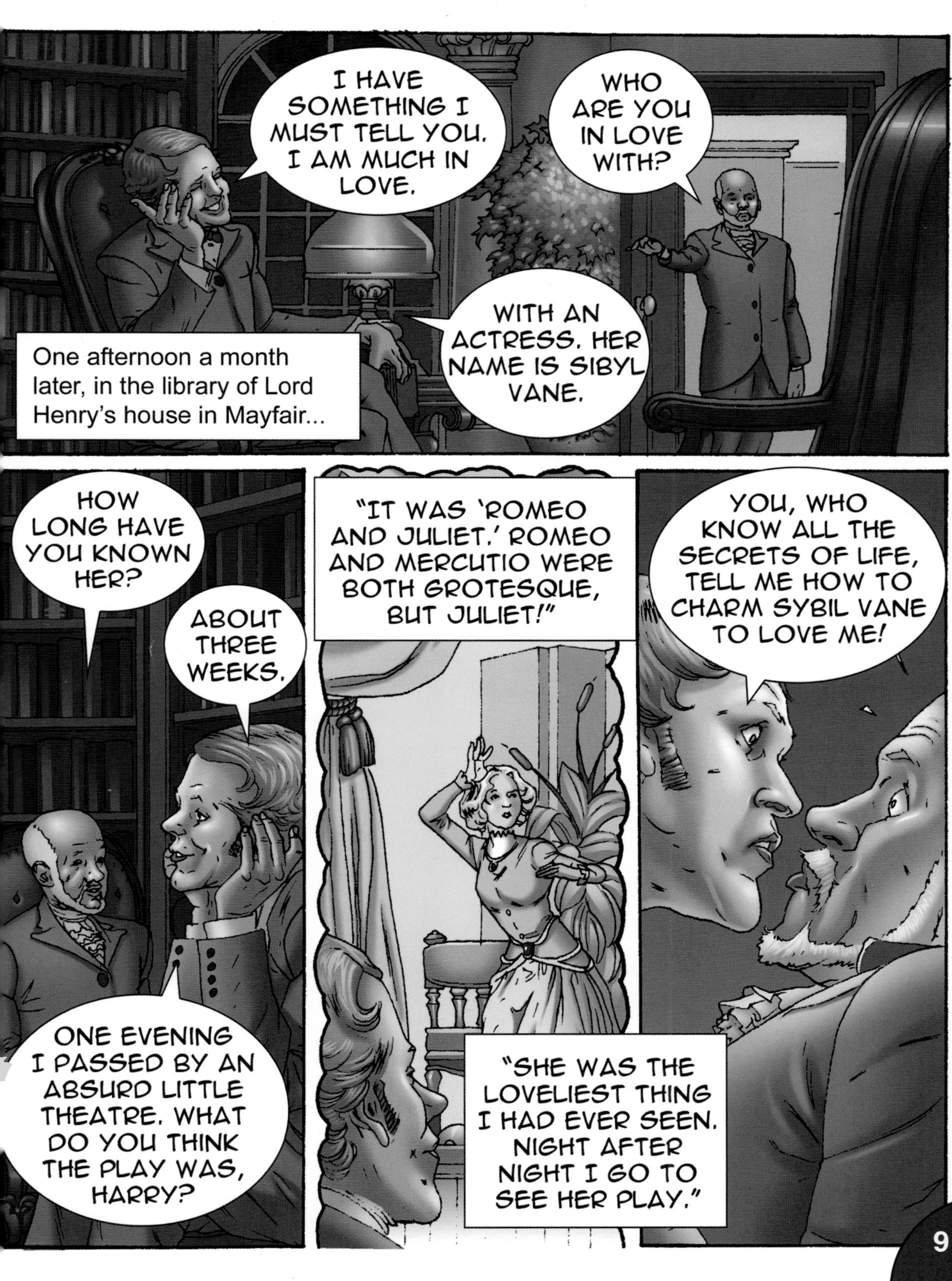
One afternoon a month later, in the library of Lord Henry's house in Mayfair...
I HAVE SOMETHING I MUST TELL YOU. I AM MUCH IN LOVE.
WHO ARE YOU IN LOVE WITH?
WITH AN ACTRESS. HER NAME IS SIBYL VANE.
HOW LONG HAVE YOU KNOWN HER?
ABOUT THREE WEEKS.
ONE EVENING I PASSED BY AN ABSURD LITTLE THEATRE. WHAT DO YOU THINK THE PLAY WAS, HARRY?
"IT WAS 'ROMEO AND JULIET.' ROMEO AND MERCUTIO WERE BOTH GROTESQUE, BUT JULIET!"
"SHE WAS THE LOVELIEST THING I HAD EVER SEEN. NIGHT AFTER NIGHT I GO TO SEE HER PLAY."
YOU, WHO KNOW ALL THE SECRETS OF LIFE, TELL ME HOW TO CHARM SYBIL VANE TO LOVE ME!

Certainly few people had ever interested Henry so much as Dorian Gray. Yet the lad's mad adoration of someone else caused him not the slightest pang of annoyance or jealousy.

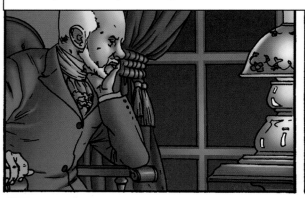

When he arrived home one afternoon several weeks later, Henry had a telegram from Dorian Gray. It was to tell him that Dorian was engaged to be married to Sibyl Vane.

Across town…

MOTHER, I AM SO HAPPY! AND YOU MUST BE HAPPY TOO!

I AM ONLY HAPPY WHEN I SEE YOU ACT. MR. ISAACS HAS BEEN VERY GOOD TO US, AND WE OWE HIM MONEY.

WHAT DOES MONEY MATTER? LOVE IS MORE THAN MONEY.

FOOLISH CHILD! WHAT DO YOU KNOW OF THIS MAN? HOWEVER, IF HE IS RICH…

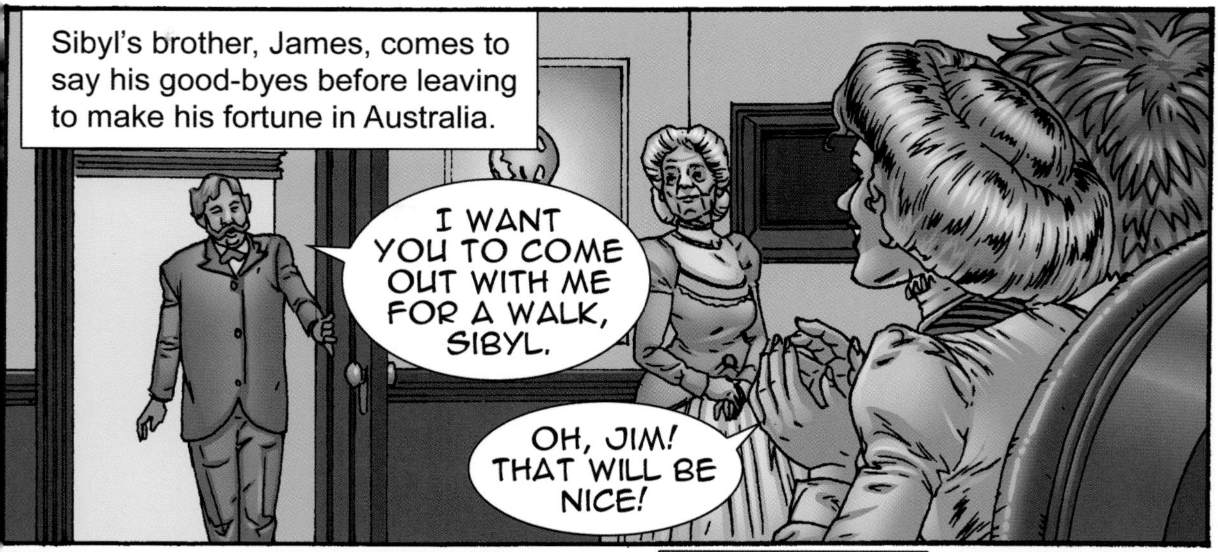
Sibyl's brother, James, comes to say his good-byes before leaving to make his fortune in Australia.
I WANT YOU TO COME OUT WITH ME FOR A WALK, SIBYL.
OH, JIM! THAT WILL BE NICE!

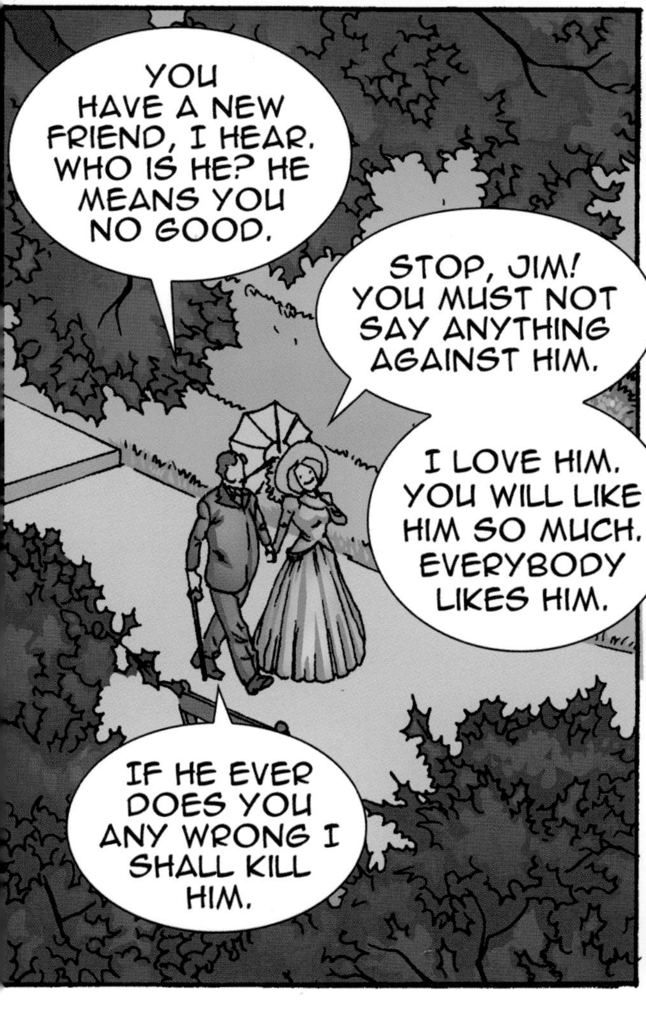
YOU HAVE A NEW FRIEND, I HEAR. WHO IS HE? HE MEANS YOU NO GOOD.
STOP, JIM! YOU MUST NOT SAY ANYTHING AGAINST HIM.
I LOVE HIM. YOU WILL LIKE HIM SO MUCH. EVERYBODY LIKES HIM.
IF HE EVER DOES YOU ANY WRONG I SHALL KILL HIM.

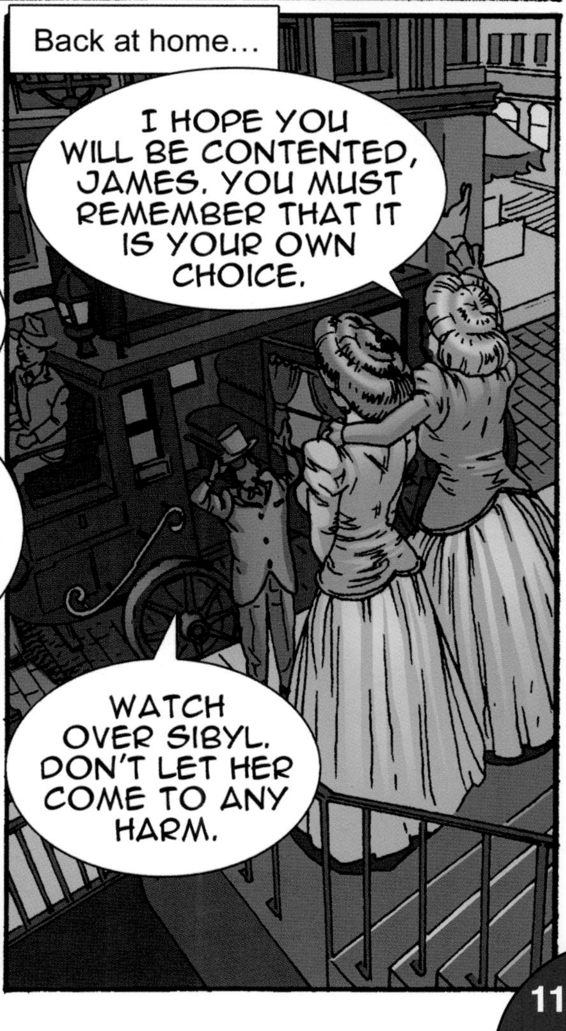
Back at home…
I HOPE YOU WILL BE CONTENTED, JAMES. YOU MUST REMEMBER THAT IT IS YOUR OWN CHOICE.
WATCH OVER SIBYL. DON'T LET HER COME TO ANY HARM.

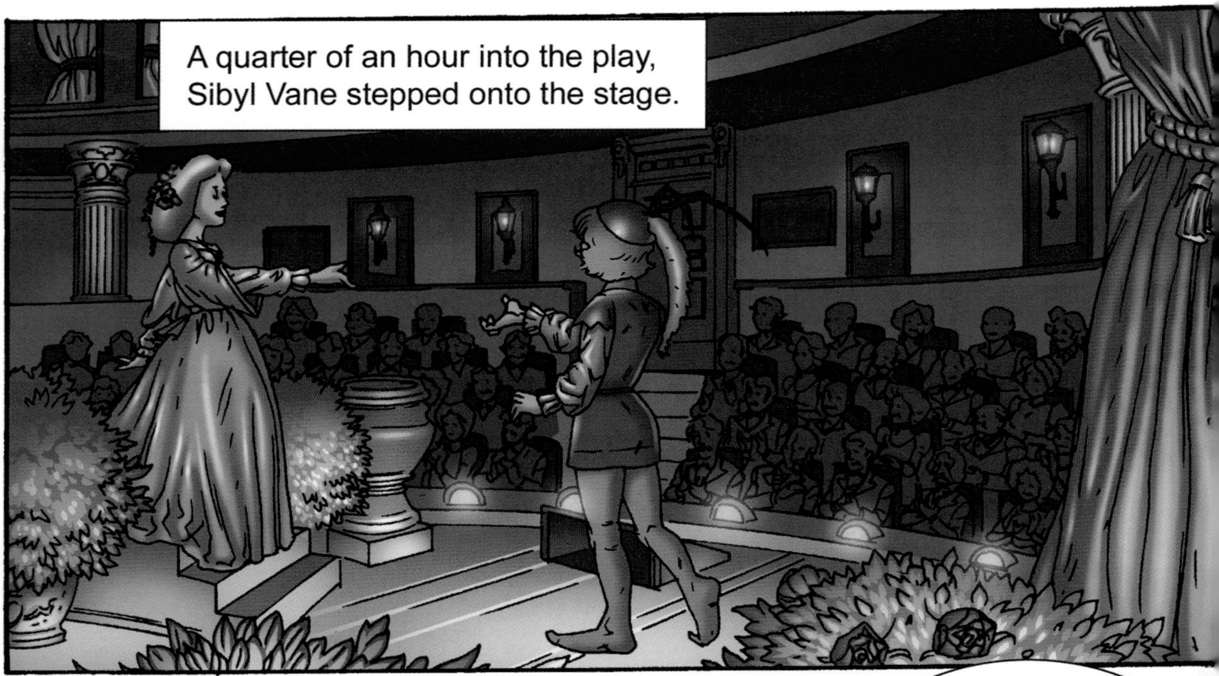
A quarter of an hour into the play, Sibyl Vane stepped onto the stage.

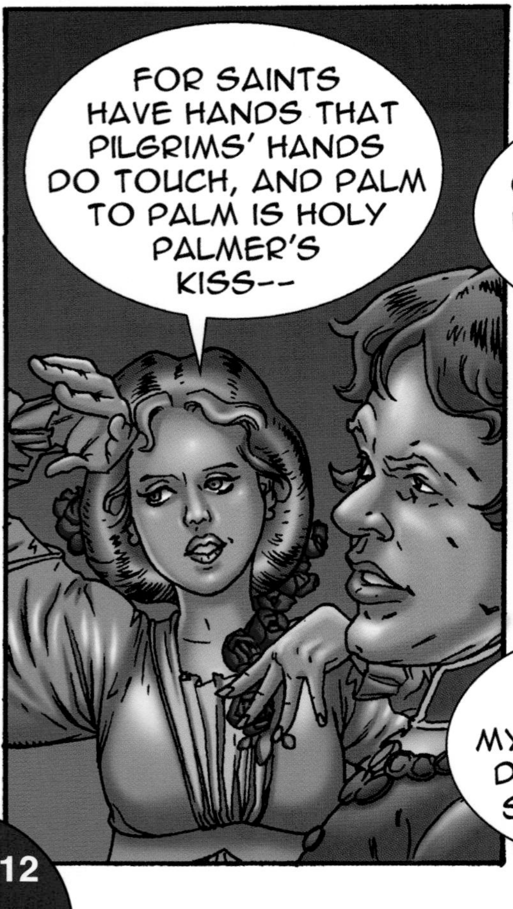
FOR SAINTS HAVE HANDS THAT PILGRIMS' HANDS DO TOUCH, AND PALM TO PALM IS HOLY PALMER'S KISS--

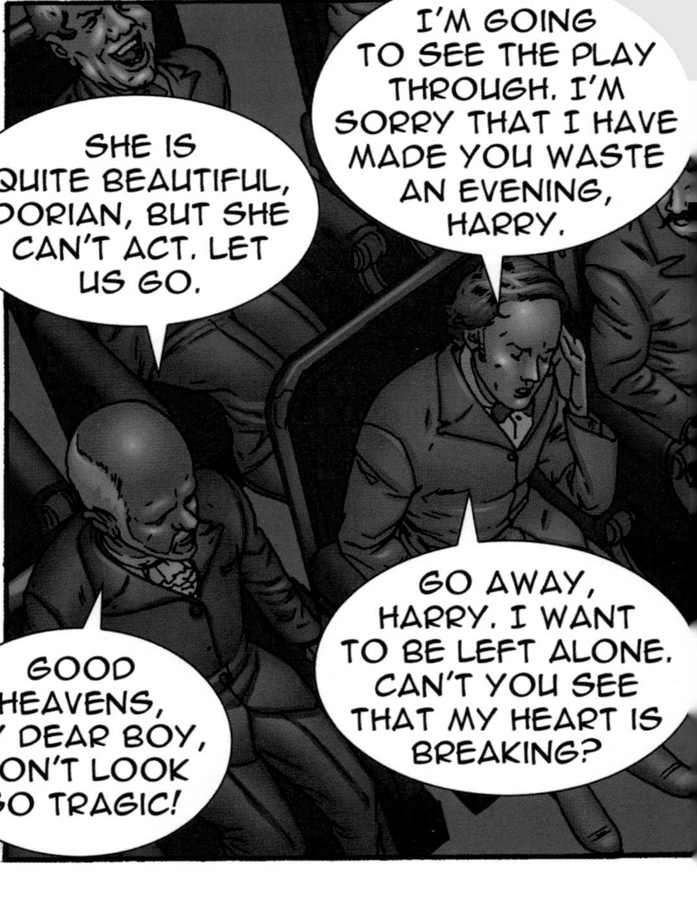
SHE IS QUITE BEAUTIFUL, DORIAN, BUT SHE CAN'T ACT. LET US GO.
I'M GOING TO SEE THE PLAY THROUGH. I'M SORRY THAT I HAVE MADE YOU WASTE AN EVENING, HARRY.
GOOD HEAVENS, MY DEAR BOY, DON'T LOOK SO TRAGIC!
GO AWAY, HARRY. I WANT TO BE LEFT ALONE. CAN'T YOU SEE THAT MY HEART IS BREAKING?

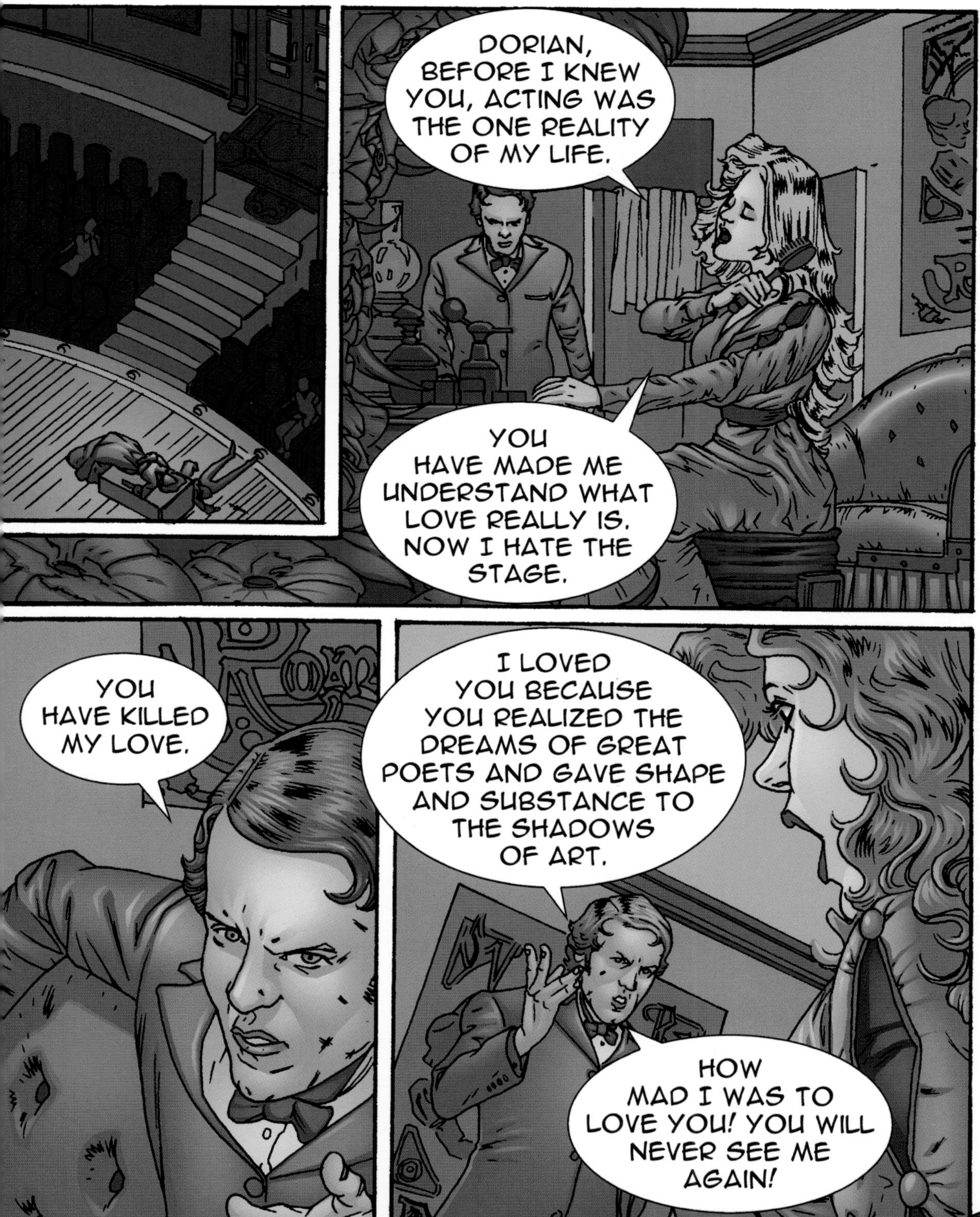
DORIAN, BEFORE I KNEW YOU, ACTING WAS THE ONE REALITY OF MY LIFE.
YOU HAVE MADE ME UNDERSTAND WHAT LOVE REALLY IS. NOW I HATE THE STAGE.
YOU HAVE KILLED MY LOVE.
I LOVED YOU BECAUSE YOU REALIZED THE DREAMS OF GREAT POETS AND GAVE SHAPE AND SUBSTANCE TO THE SHADOWS OF ART.
HOW MAD I WAS TO LOVE YOU! YOU WILL NEVER SEE ME AGAIN!

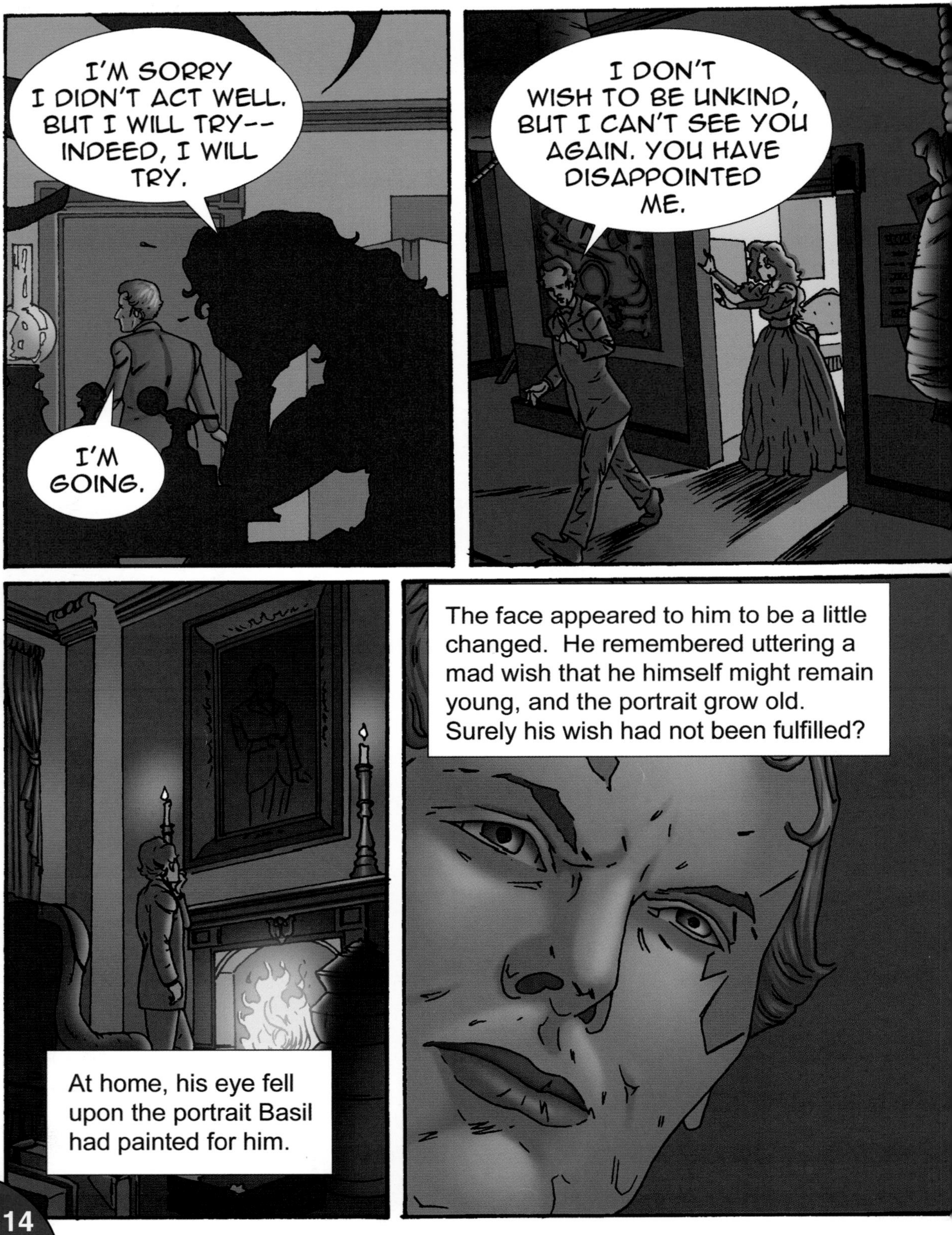
I'M SORRY I DIDN'T ACT WELL. BUT I WILL TRY-- INDEED, I WILL TRY.
I'M GOING.
I DON'T WISH TO BE UNKIND, BUT I CAN'T SEE YOU AGAIN. YOU HAVE DISAPPOINTED ME.
At home, his eye fell upon the portrait Basil had painted for him.
The face appeared to him to be a little changed. He remembered uttering a mad wish that he himself might remain young, and the portrait grow old. Surely his wish had not been fulfilled?

The next day, Lord Henry entered Dorian's library…

YOUR WIFE! DIDN'T YOU GET MY LETTER? SIBYL VANE IS DEAD!

DEAD! IT'S A HORRIBLE LIE! HOW DARE YOU SAY IT?

IT IS QUITE TRUE, DORIAN. THEY FOUND HER ON THE FLOOR OF HER DRESSING ROOM.

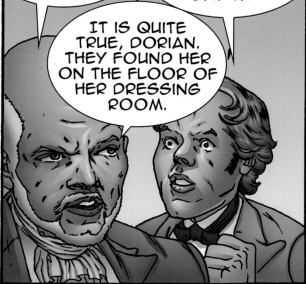

I WAS BRUTAL, HARRY. BUT TWO DAYS AGO I ASKED SIBYL TO MARRY ME. I AM NOT GOING TO BREAK MY WORD TO HER. SHE IS TO BE MY WIFE!

I HAVE MURDERED SIBYL VANE. MURDERED HER AS SURELY AS IF I HAD CUT HER LITTLE THROAT WITH A KNIFE.

BUT WE WILL NOT TALK AGAIN OF WHAT HAS HAPPENED. I WONDER IF LIFE HAS STILL IN STORE FOR ME ANYTHING AS MARVELOUS.

LIFE HAS EVERYTHING IN STORE FOR YOU, DORIAN.

Eternal youth, secret pleasures, wild joys, and wilder sins—he was to have all of these things.

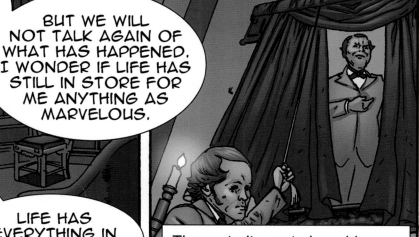

The portrait was to bear his shame. The portrait would be to him the most magical of mirrors.

15

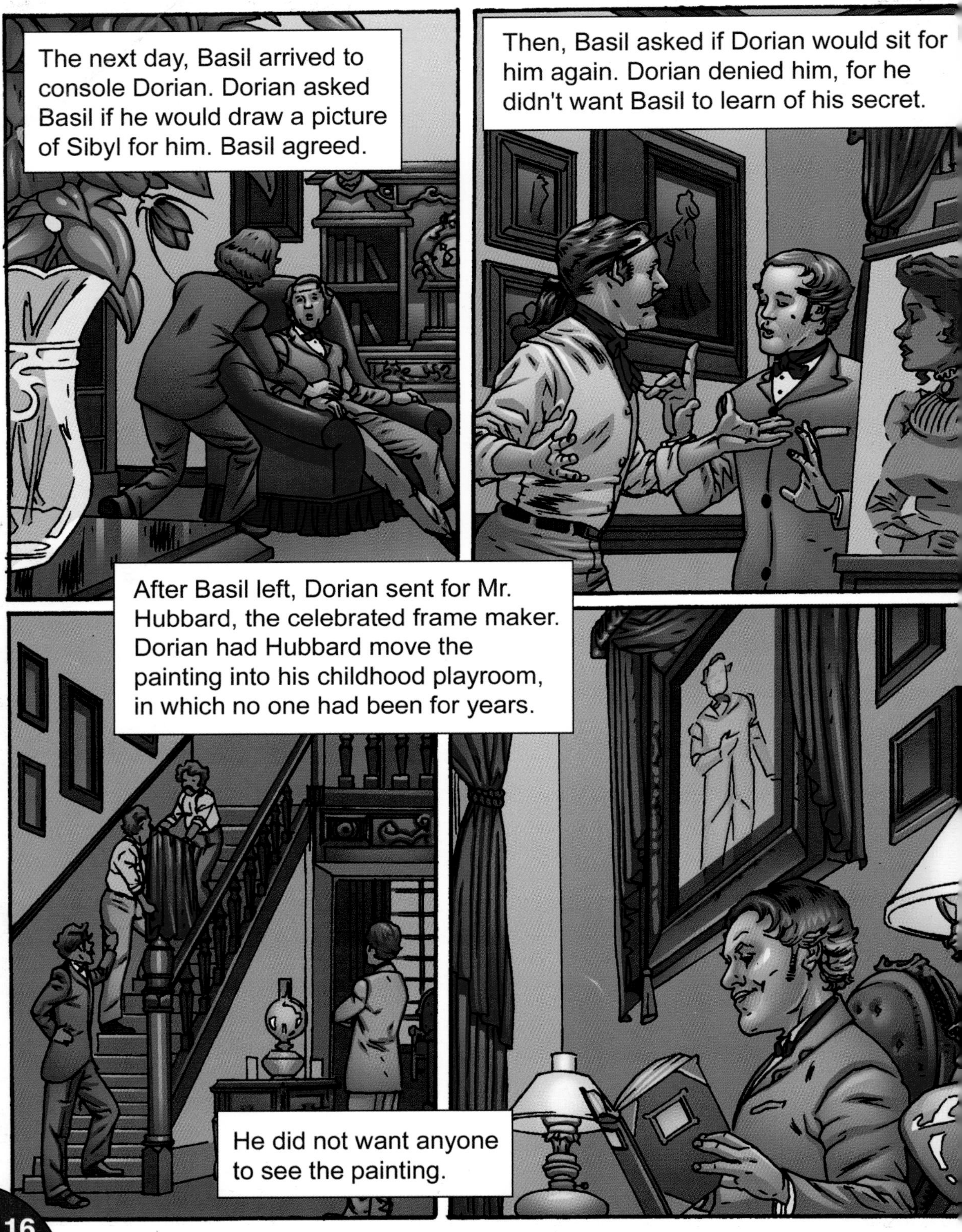
The next day, Basil arrived to console Dorian. Dorian asked Basil if he would draw a picture of Sibyl for him. Basil agreed.
Then, Basil asked if Dorian would sit for him again. Dorian denied him, for he didn't want Basil to learn of his secret.
After Basil left, Dorian sent for Mr. Hubbard, the celebrated frame maker. Dorian had Hubbard move the painting into his childhood playroom, in which no one had been for years.
He did not want anyone to see the painting.

For years, the wonderful beauty that had so fascinated Basil and many others besides him seemed never to leave Dorian.

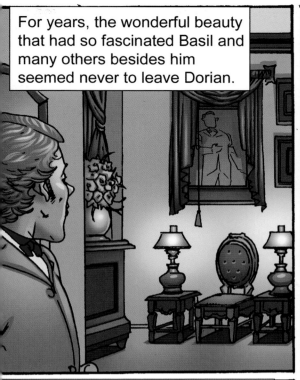

Even those who had heard the most evil things against him could not believe anything to his dishonor when they saw him.

Often, Dorian would creep upstairs and stand in front of the portrait. He would look at the evil, aging face on the canvas. Then he would gaze at the fair young face that laughed back at him from a mirror.

He grew more interested in the corruption of his own soul. Curious stories about him became common after he passed his twenty-fifth year.

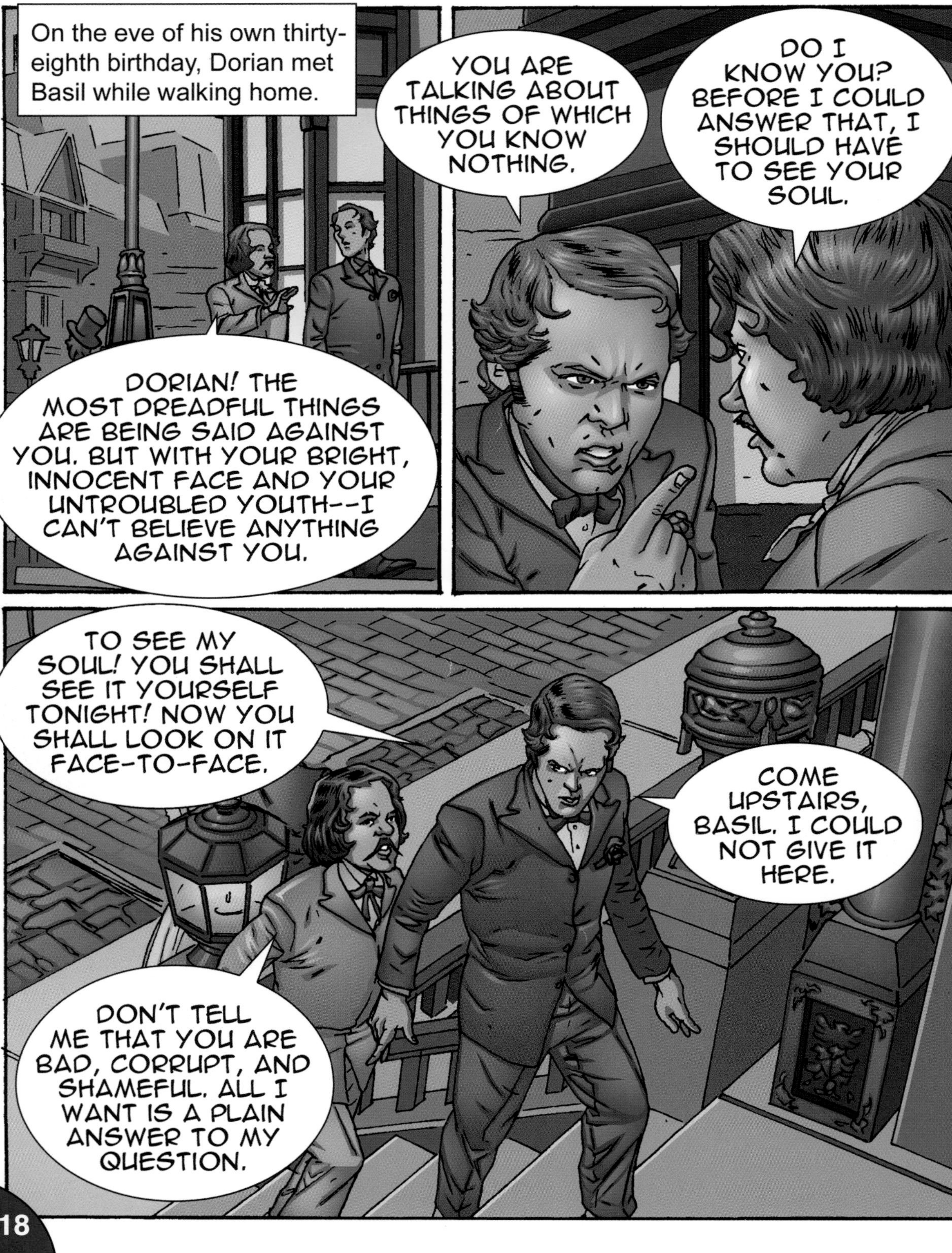
On the eve of his own thirty-eighth birthday, Dorian met Basil while walking home.
DORIAN! THE MOST DREADFUL THINGS ARE BEING SAID AGAINST YOU. BUT WITH YOUR BRIGHT, INNOCENT FACE AND YOUR UNTROUBLED YOUTH--I CAN'T BELIEVE ANYTHING AGAINST YOU.
YOU ARE TALKING ABOUT THINGS OF WHICH YOU KNOW NOTHING.
DO I KNOW YOU? BEFORE I COULD ANSWER THAT, I SHOULD HAVE TO SEE YOUR SOUL.
TO SEE MY SOUL! YOU SHALL SEE IT YOURSELF TONIGHT! NOW YOU SHALL LOOK ON IT FACE-TO-FACE.
COME UPSTAIRS, BASIL. I COULD NOT GIVE IT HERE.
DON'T TELL ME THAT YOU ARE BAD, CORRUPT, AND SHAMEFUL. ALL I WANT IS A PLAIN ANSWER TO MY QUESTION.

BASIL, YOU ARE THE ONE MAN IN THE WORLD WHO IS ENTITLED TO KNOW EVERYTHING ABOUT ME.

YOU HAD MORE TO DO WITH MY LIFE THAN YOU THINK. SHUT THE DOOR.

It was Dorian Gray's own face that he was looking at! The horror, whatever it was, had not yet entirely spoiled the marvelous beauty.

It was Basil's own picture. He knew it. Why had it altered?

WHAT DOES THIS MEAN?

YEARS AGO, YOU MET ME, FLATTERED ME, AND TAUGHT ME TO BE VAIN OF MY GOOD LOOKS. YOU FINISHED THE PORTRAIT OF ME THAT REVEALED TO ME THE WONDER OF BEAUTY.

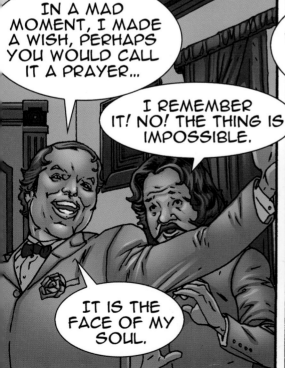

IN A MAD MOMENT, I MADE A WISH, PERHAPS YOU WOULD CALL IT A PRAYER...

I REMEMBER IT! NO! THE THING IS IMPOSSIBLE.

IT IS THE FACE OF MY SOUL.

IF IT IS TRUE YOU MUST BE WORSE EVEN THAN THOSE WHO TALK AGAINST YOU FANCY YOU TO BE!

HUSH! DON'T YOU SEE THAT ACCURSED THING LEERING AT US?

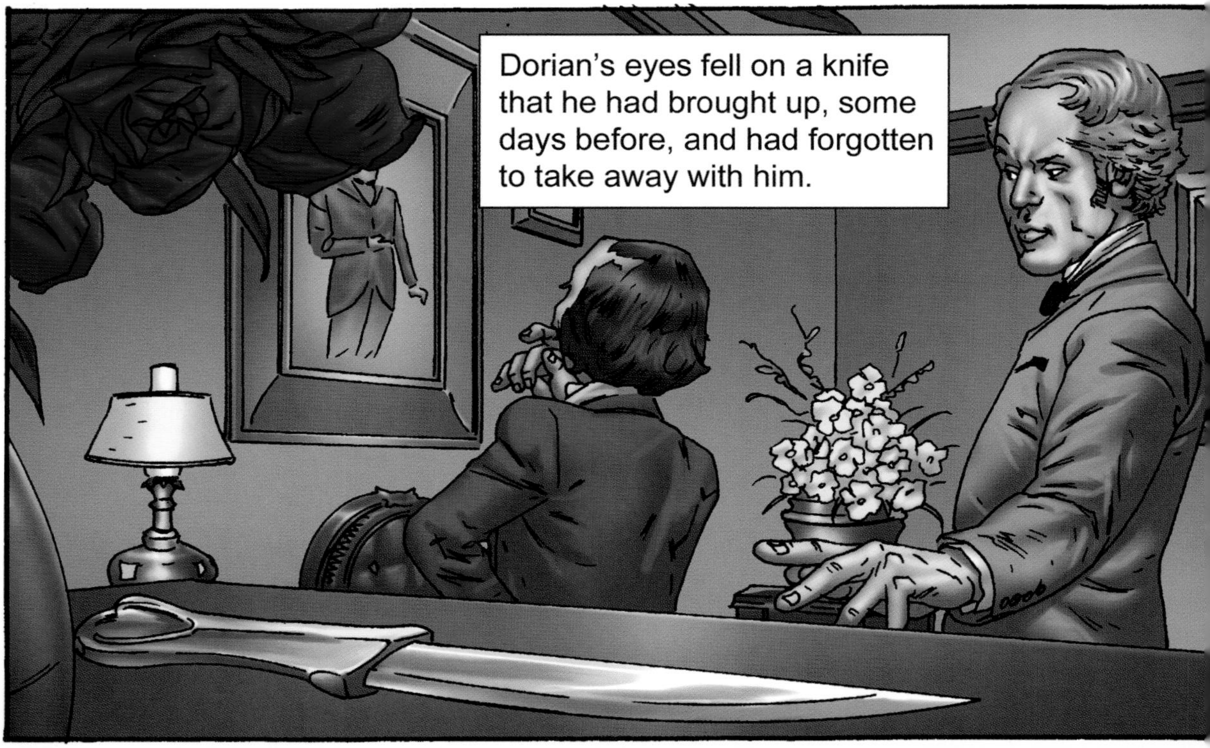
Dorian's eyes fell on a knife that he had brought up, some days before, and had forgotten to take away with him.

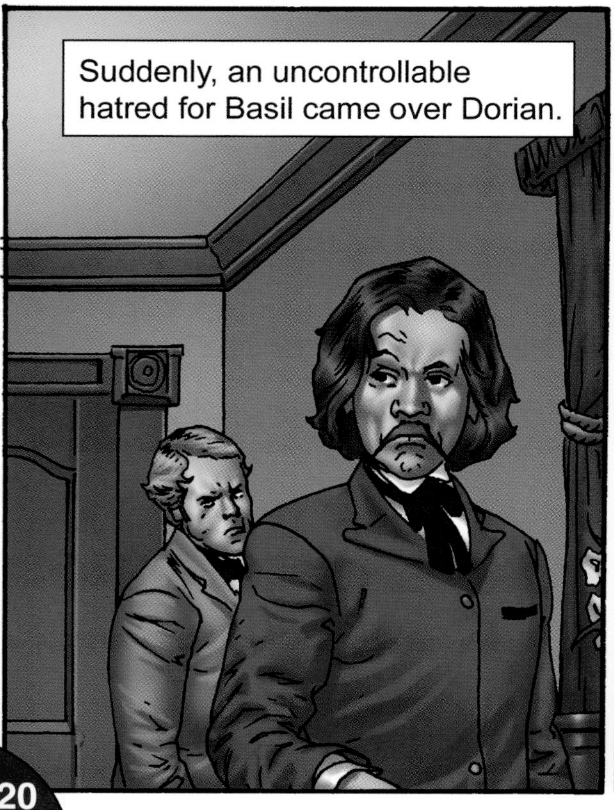
Suddenly, an uncontrollable hatred for Basil came over Dorian.

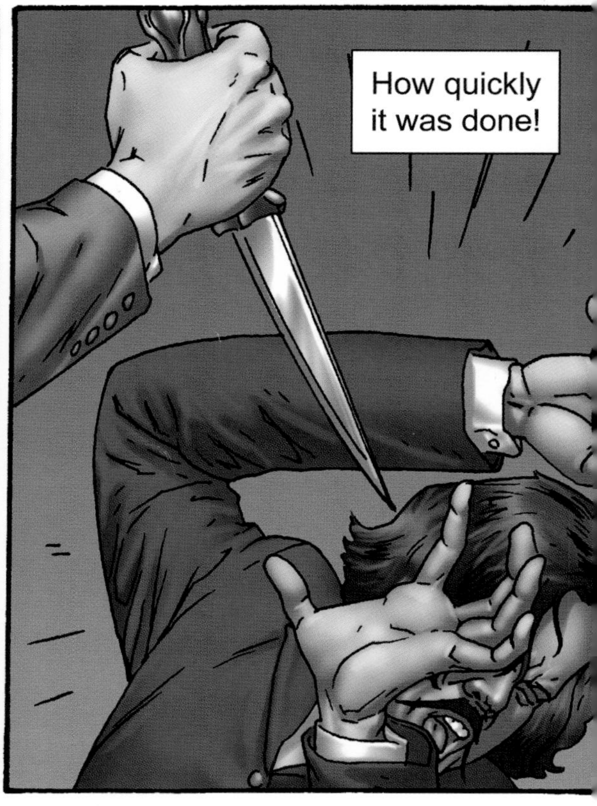
How quickly it was done!

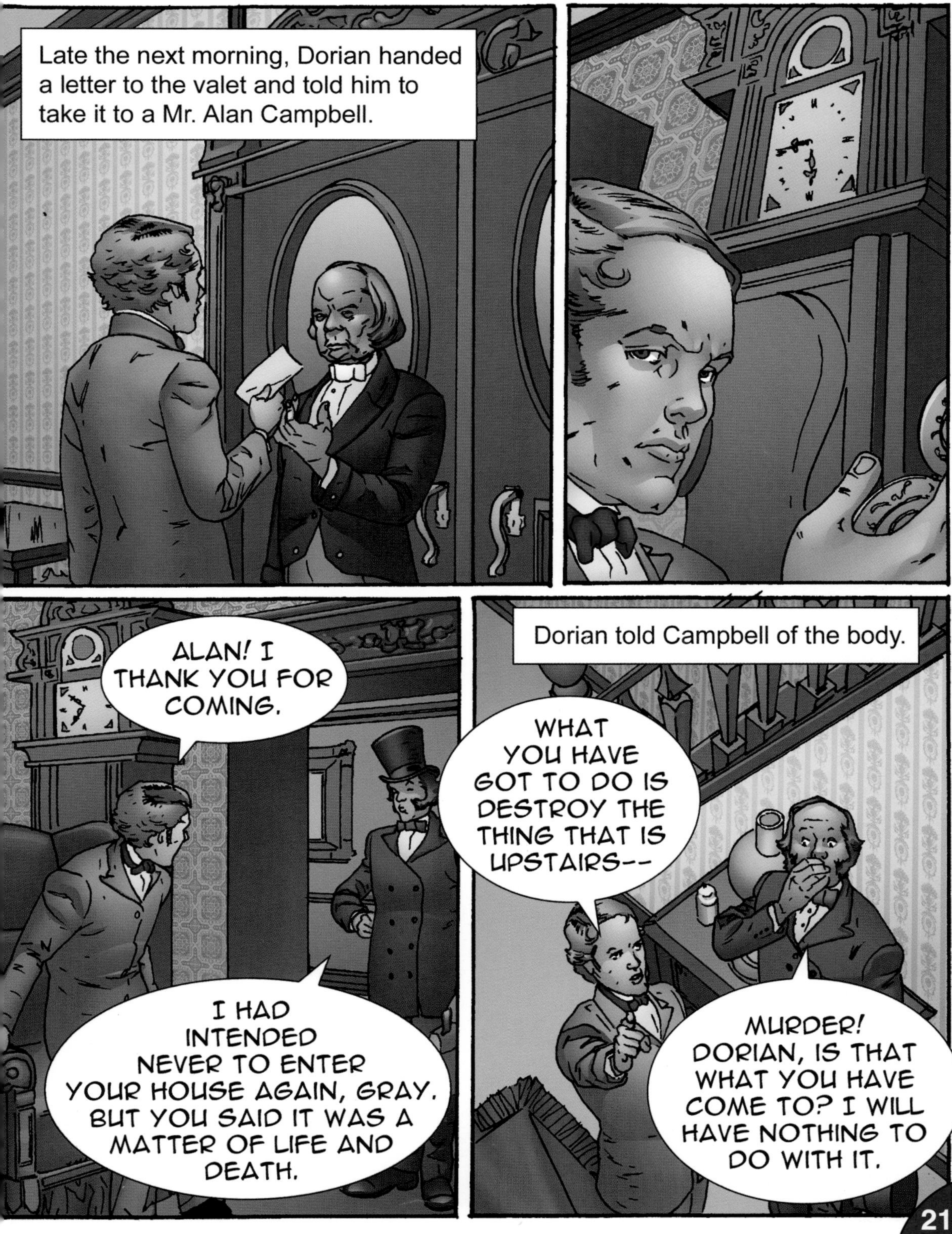
Late the next morning, Dorian handed a letter to the valet and told him to take it to a Mr. Alan Campbell.
ALAN! I THANK YOU FOR COMING.
I HAD INTENDED NEVER TO ENTER YOUR HOUSE AGAIN, GRAY. BUT YOU SAID IT WAS A MATTER OF LIFE AND DEATH.
Dorian told Campbell of the body.
WHAT YOU HAVE GOT TO DO IS DESTROY THE THING THAT IS UPSTAIRS--
MURDER! DORIAN, IS THAT WHAT YOU HAVE COME TO? I WILL HAVE NOTHING TO DO WITH IT.

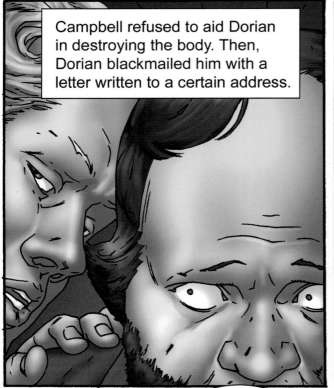

Campbell refused to aid Dorian in destroying the body. Then, Dorian blackmailed him with a letter written to a certain address.

I HAVE DONE WHAT YOU ASKED ME TO DO. AND NOW, GOOD-BYE. LET US NEVER SEE EACH OTHER AGAIN.

YOU HAVE SAVED ME FROM RUIN, ALAN.

There was a horrible smell in the room. But the thing that had been sitting at the table was gone.

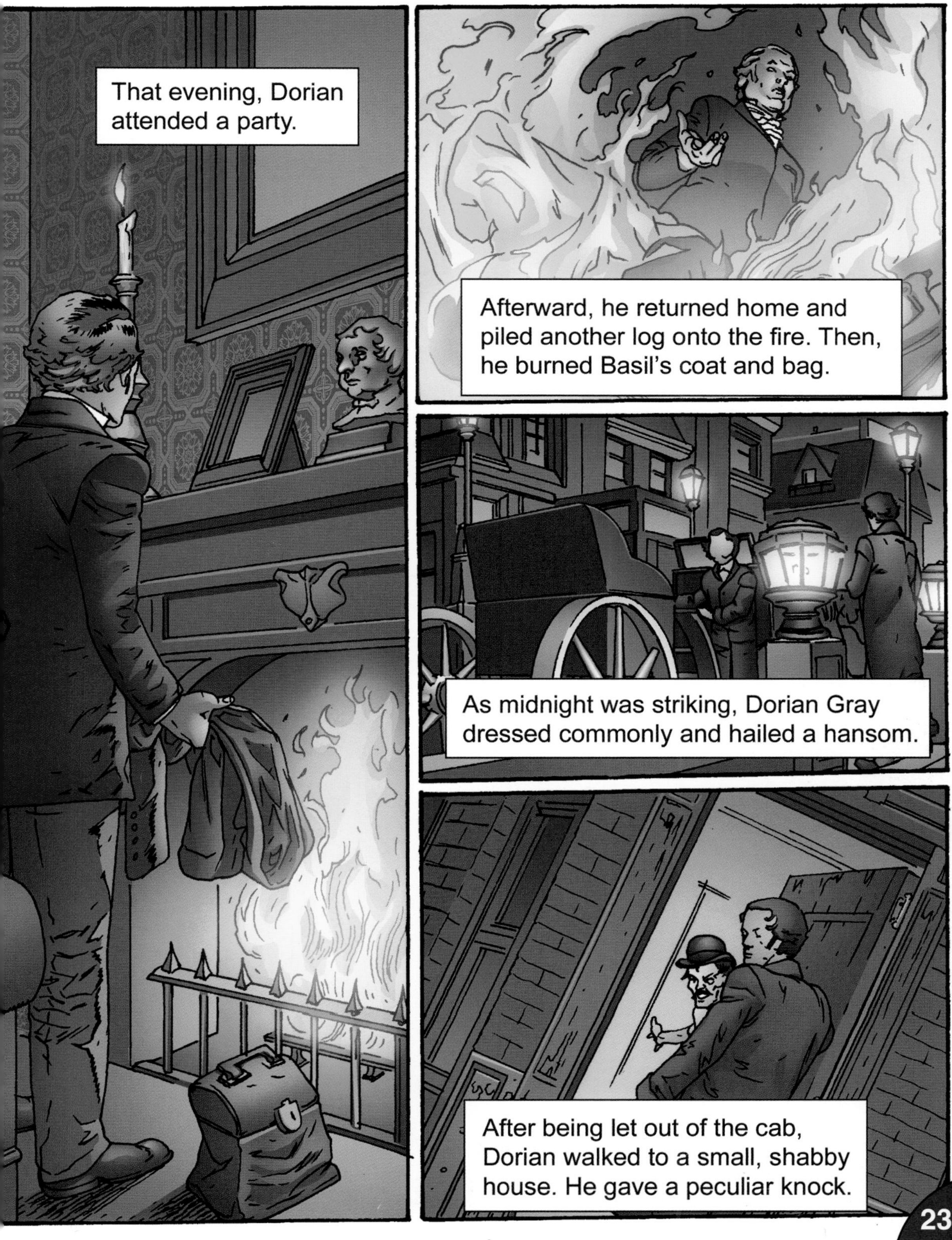
That evening, Dorian attended a party.
Afterward, he returned home and piled another log onto the fire. Then, he burned Basil's coat and bag.
As midnight was striking, Dorian Gray dressed commonly and hailed a hansom.
After being let out of the cab, Dorian walked to a small, shabby house. He gave a peculiar knock.

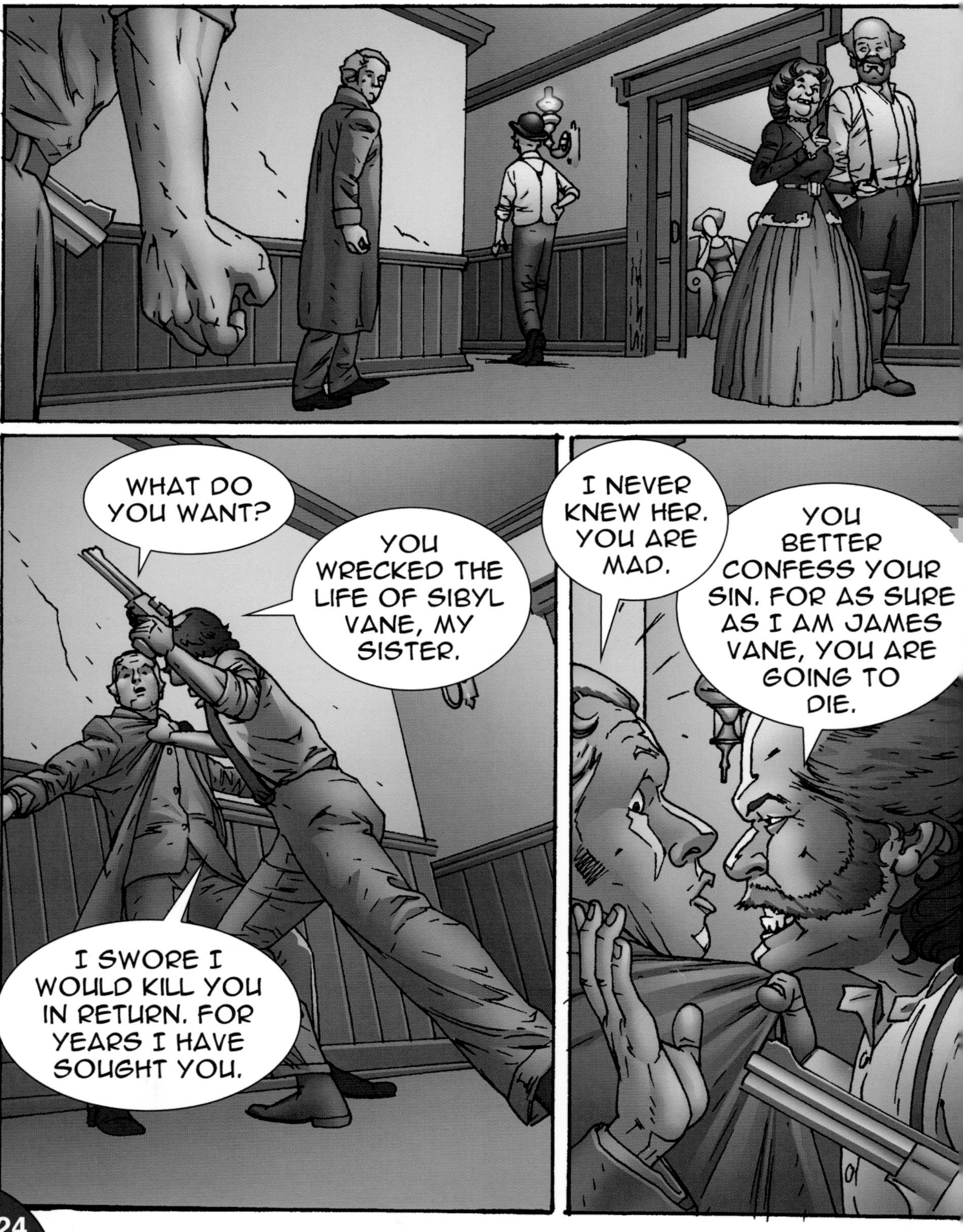
WHAT DO YOU WANT?
YOU WRECKED THE LIFE OF SIBYL VANE, MY SISTER.
I SWORE I WOULD KILL YOU IN RETURN. FOR YEARS I HAVE SOUGHT YOU.
I NEVER KNEW HER. YOU ARE MAD.
YOU BETTER CONFESS YOUR SIN. FOR AS SURE AS I AM JAMES VANE, YOU ARE GOING TO DIE.

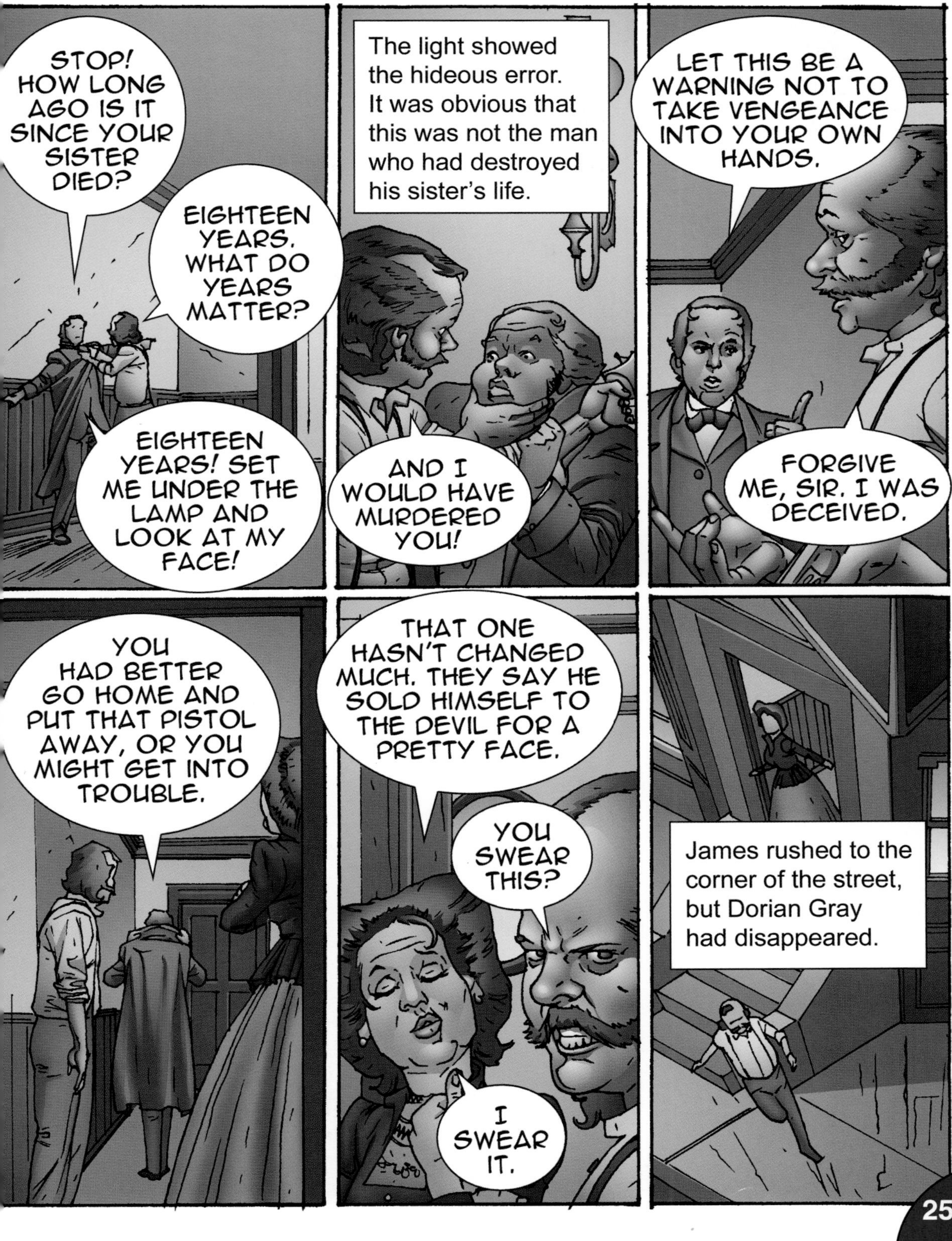
STOP! HOW LONG AGO IS IT SINCE YOUR SISTER DIED?
EIGHTEEN YEARS. WHAT DO YEARS MATTER?
EIGHTEEN YEARS! SET ME UNDER THE LAMP AND LOOK AT MY FACE!
The light showed the hideous error. It was obvious that this was not the man who had destroyed his sister's life.
AND I WOULD HAVE MURDERED YOU!
LET THIS BE A WARNING NOT TO TAKE VENGEANCE INTO YOUR OWN HANDS.
FORGIVE ME, SIR. I WAS DECEIVED.
YOU HAD BETTER GO HOME AND PUT THAT PISTOL AWAY, OR YOU MIGHT GET INTO TROUBLE.
THAT ONE HASN'T CHANGED MUCH. THEY SAY HE SOLD HIMSELF TO THE DEVIL FOR A PRETTY FACE.
YOU SWEAR THIS?
I SWEAR IT.
James rushed to the corner of the street, but Dorian Gray had disappeared.

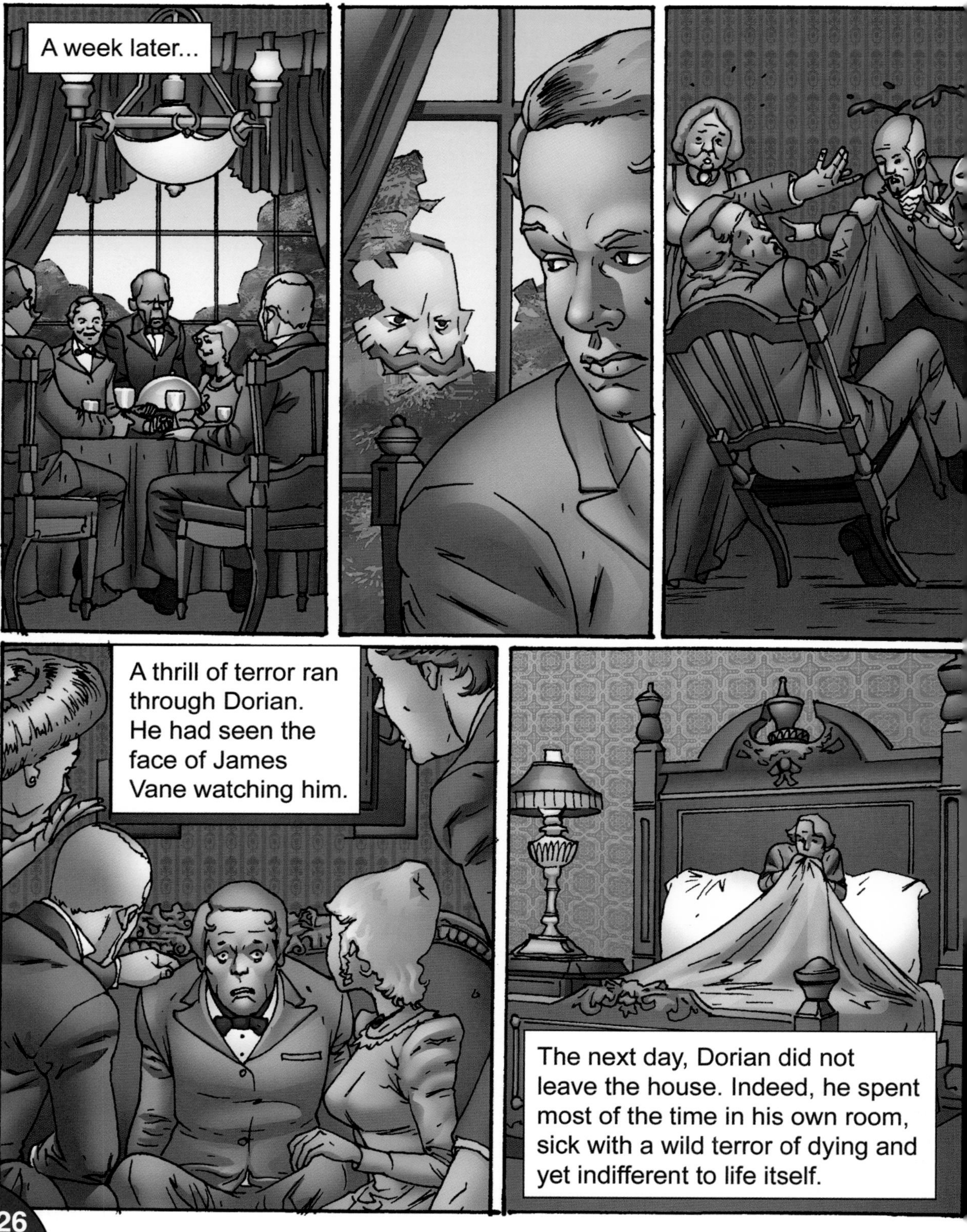
A week later...
A thrill of terror ran through Dorian. He had seen the face of James Vane watching him.
The next day, Dorian did not leave the house. Indeed, he spent most of the time in his own room, sick with a wild terror of dying and yet indifferent to life itself.

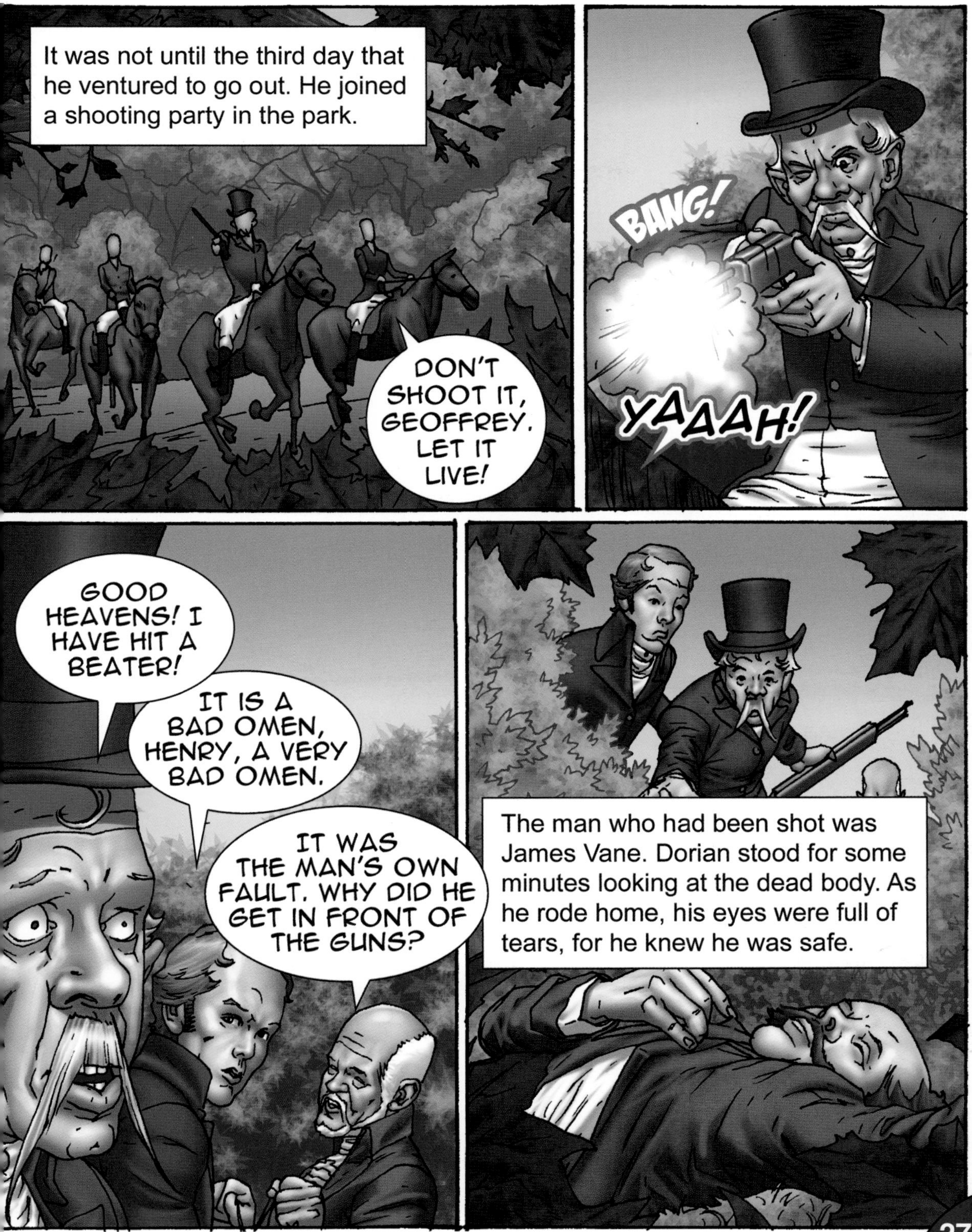
It was not until the third day that he ventured to go out. He joined a shooting party in the park.
DON'T SHOOT IT, GEOFFREY. LET IT LIVE!
BANG!
YAAAH!
GOOD HEAVENS! I HAVE HIT A BEATER!
IT IS A BAD OMEN, HENRY, A VERY BAD OMEN.
IT WAS THE MAN'S OWN FAULT. WHY DID HE GET IN FRONT OF THE GUNS?
The man who had been shot was James Vane. Dorian stood for some minutes looking at the dead body. As he rode home, his eyes were full of tears, for he knew he was safe.

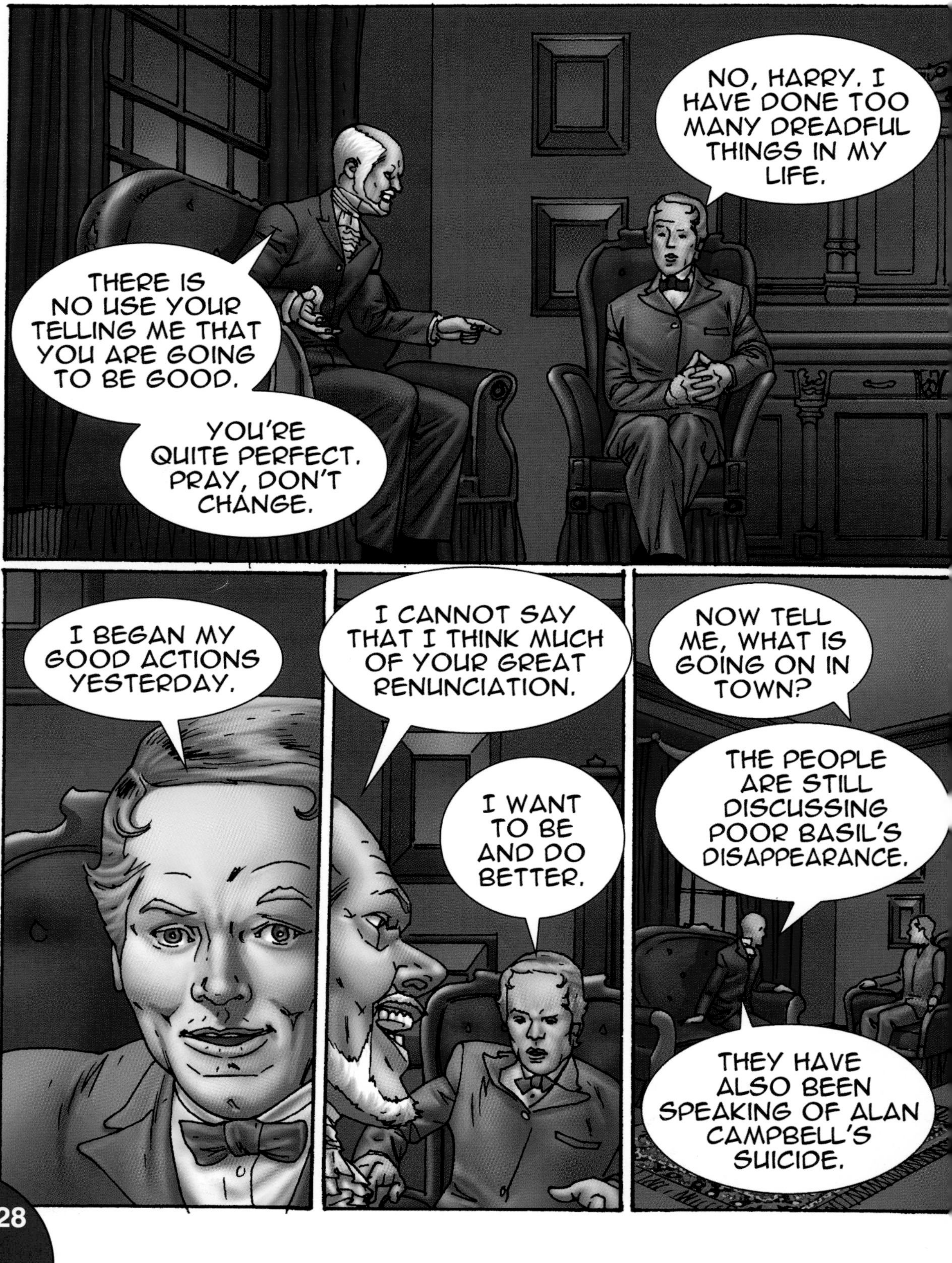
NO, HARRY. I HAVE DONE TOO MANY DREADFUL THINGS IN MY LIFE.
THERE IS NO USE YOUR TELLING ME THAT YOU ARE GOING TO BE GOOD.
YOU'RE QUITE PERFECT. PRAY, DON'T CHANGE.
I BEGAN MY GOOD ACTIONS YESTERDAY.
I CANNOT SAY THAT I THINK MUCH OF YOUR GREAT RENUNCIATION.
I WANT TO BE AND DO BETTER.
NOW TELL ME, WHAT IS GOING ON IN TOWN?
THE PEOPLE ARE STILL DISCUSSING POOR BASIL'S DISAPPEARANCE.
THEY HAVE ALSO BEEN SPEAKING OF ALAN CAMPBELL'S SUICIDE.

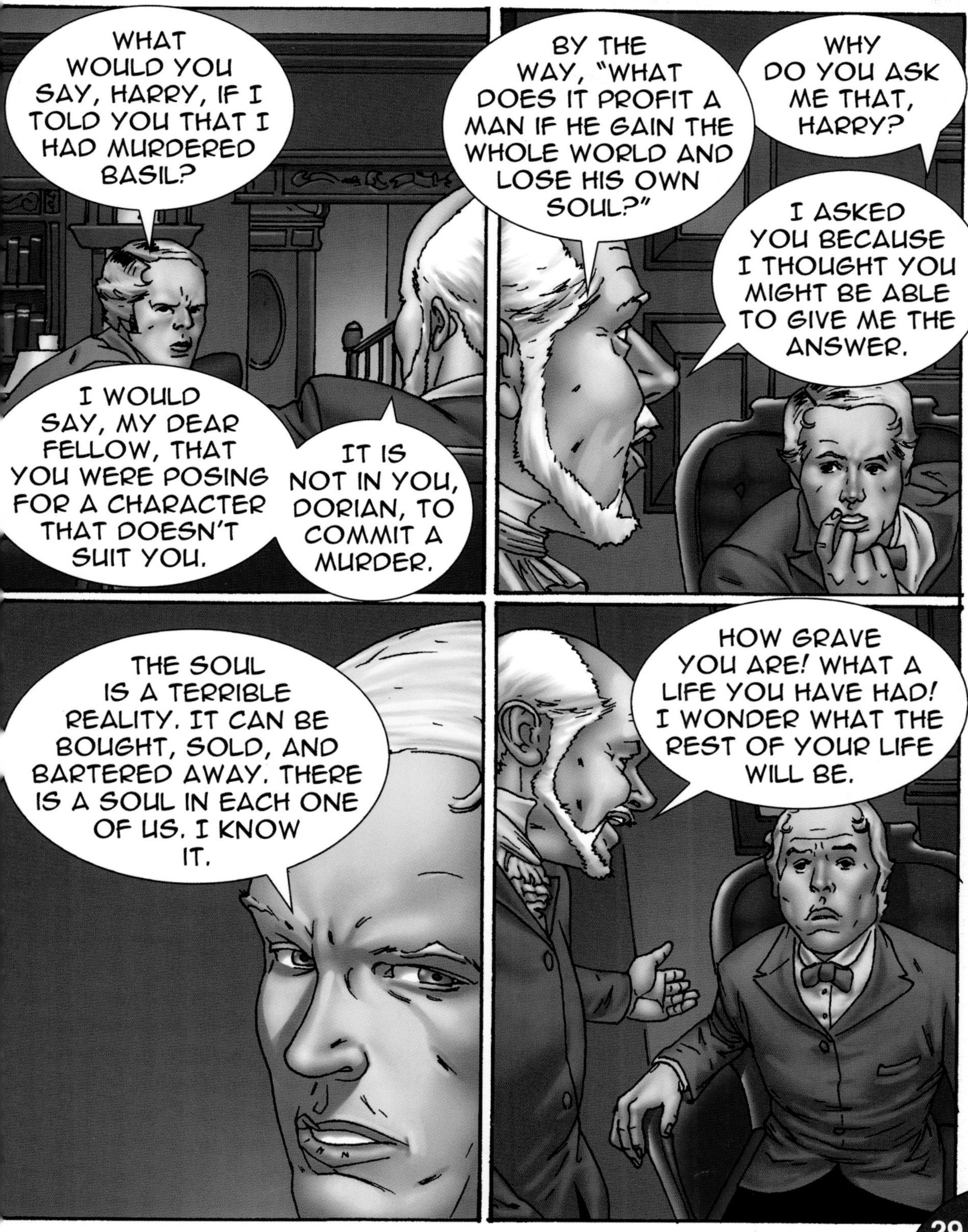

WHAT WOULD YOU SAY, HARRY, IF I TOLD YOU THAT I HAD MURDERED BASIL?
I WOULD SAY, MY DEAR FELLOW, THAT YOU WERE POSING FOR A CHARACTER THAT DOESN'T SUIT YOU.
IT IS NOT IN YOU, DORIAN, TO COMMIT A MURDER.
BY THE WAY, "WHAT DOES IT PROFIT A MAN IF HE GAIN THE WHOLE WORLD AND LOSE HIS OWN SOUL?"
WHY DO YOU ASK ME THAT, HARRY?
I ASKED YOU BECAUSE I THOUGHT YOU MIGHT BE ABLE TO GIVE ME THE ANSWER.
THE SOUL IS A TERRIBLE REALITY. IT CAN BE BOUGHT, SOLD, AND BARTERED AWAY. THERE IS A SOUL IN EACH ONE OF US. I KNOW IT.
HOW GRAVE YOU ARE! WHAT A LIFE YOU HAVE HAD! I WONDER WHAT THE REST OF YOUR LIFE WILL BE.

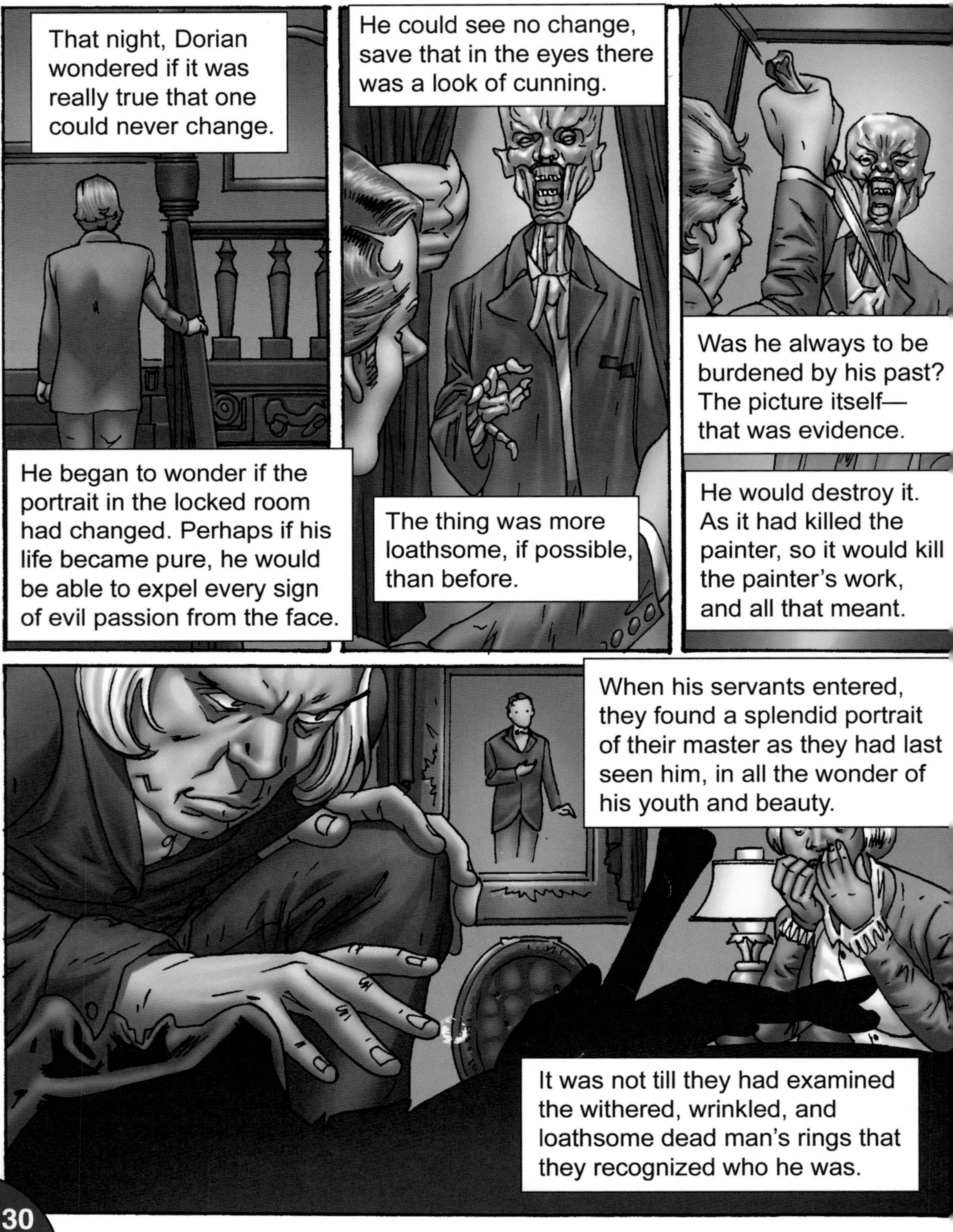
That night, Dorian wondered if it was really true that one could never change.
He began to wonder if the portrait in the locked room had changed. Perhaps if his life became pure, he would be able to expel every sign of evil passion from the face.
He could see no change, save that in the eyes there was a look of cunning.
The thing was more loathsome, if possible, than before.
Was he always to be burdened by his past? The picture itself—that was evidence.
He would destroy it. As it had killed the painter, so it would kill the painter's work, and all that meant.
When his servants entered, they found a splendid portrait of their master as they had last seen him, in all the wonder of his youth and beauty.
It was not till they had examined the withered, wrinkled, and loathsome dead man's rings that they recognized who he was.

About the Author

Oscar Fingal O'Flahertie Wills Wilde was born on October 16, 1854, in Dublin Ireland. His father, Sir William Wilde, was Ireland's leading eye surgeon. His mother was a revolutionary poet who wrote under the name Speranza.

Wilde attended schools in Ireland and England. During his years of schooling, Wilde established himself as a scholar and poet. In 1878, he earned a degree with honors from Magdalen College. That year, he also won the Newdigate Prize for his long poem *Ravenna*.

In 1881, Wilde published a collection of poems at his own expense called *Poems*. He then traveled to the United States in 1882. He returned to Great Britain a year later. Wilde married Constance Lloyd in 1884 and had two children, Cyril and Vyvyan.

Wilde worked as a review and editor and continued to write poetry. He wrote only one novel, *The Picture of Dorian Gray*, in 1891. He then began writing for the theater, where he found more success.

Oscar Wilde died suddenly on November 30, 1900, in Paris, France. Today, Wilde is remembered for his poetry, plays, and tales of mystery and death. He remains an important influence on many writers.

Additional Works

Ravenna (1878)
Poems (1881)
The Happy Prince and Other Tales (1888)
The Picture of Dorian Gray (1891)
Intentions (1891)
Lady Windermere's Fan (1892)
An Ideal Husband (1895)
The Importance of Being Earnest (1895)

Glossary

beater - a person who beats bushes and plants so that animals hiding will come out into the open.

corrupt - showing dishonest or improper behavior.

cunning - showing sly or crafty behavior.

dreadful - extremely unpleasant or shocking.

grotesque - extremely ugly.

hideous - extremely ugly.

passion - strong feelings.

renunciation - the act of giving up or refusing to act a certain way.

suicide - the act of taking one's own life.

valet - a man's male servant who performs personal services.

vengeance - a punishment for an injury or offense.

Web Sites

To learn more about Oscar Wilde, visit the ABDO Group online at **www.abdopublishing.com**. Web sites about Wilde are featured on our Book Links page. These links are routinely monitored and updated to provide the most current information available.